# ANNY COOK,
## Dancer's Delight

## Cerridwen Press

# *What the critics are saying...*

&

**5 Angels** "Dancer's Delight is just that—a delight! Anny Cook has written a fabulous story, complete with transitions between the everyday world and another, more intriguing, world. [...]Anny Cook has conjured a world that is filled with amazing characters and a valley that is so inviting, I'd love to live there myself! [...]I really enjoyed reading this book. It is entertaining and the hours flew by!" ~ *Fallen Angels Reviews*

"I read through this in one day because I didn't want to put it down. To be honest the compulsion didn't have to do with the main characters. [...] I found myself drawn to the side characters as strongly as her hero and heroine. [...] The story of Eppie's brothers Llyon and Tyger is touching and sweetly painful to watch unfold. While it's hard to push aside social mores, it is obvious that this is a bonding of souls that defies convention." ~ *Jae's Blog – Book Reviews*

*Dear Kelly,*
*Sister of my heart,*
*I love you girl,*
*Anny Cook*

A Cerridwen Press Publication

www.cerridwenpress.com

Dancer's Delight

# Also by Anny Cook

ဢ

*If you are interested in a spicier read (and are over 18), check out the author's erotic romances at Ellora's Cave Publishing (www.ellorascave.com).*

Cherished Destinies
Chrysanthemum
Everything Lovers Can Know
Traveller's Refuge
Winter Hearts

# About the Author

๛

Anny Cook learned to read at five years old. Learning to write was a natural extension. Through her adult years while a wife, mother, grandmother, fast food cook, warehouse book packer, Girl Scout and Cub Scout Leader, perpetual college student, executive secretary, and adult education teacher, writing served as the anchor that kept her sane.

Well, maybe not exactly sane, but close to it. Today, after thirty-five years with kids, cats, dogs, guinea pigs, and hamsters, she and her husband are empty nesters. Sigh. Finally, there's time—and quiet—to write in peace.

Anny welcomes comments from readers. You can find her website and email address on her author bio page at www.cerridwenpress.com.

## Tell Us What You Think

We appreciate hearing reader opinions about our books. You can email us at Comments@EllorasCave.com.

# DANCER'S DELIGHT

ა

# Dedication

ஐ

*For Dorian, who was there in the beginning when I needed encouragement; for Terry, who was there in the middle to read all the first attempts; for Jane, who was there that night and shared my joy when I received my first offer of a contract for this book; and especially for Dan, who always understood that writing was more important than dishes, laundry, and cooking dinner — but not lovemaking.*

# Trademarks Acknowledgement

ஐ

The author acknowledges the trademarked status and trademark owners of the following wordmarks mentioned in this work of fiction:

Aleve: Syntex Puerto Rico, Inc. Corporation

Boy Scouts: Boy Scouts of America

Explorer: Ford Motor Company Corporation

Jeep: DaimlerChrysler Corporation

McDonald's: McDonald's Corporation

Nikes: Nike, Incorporated Corporation

Vulcan: Paramount Pictures Corporation

Wal-Mart: Wal-Mart Stores, Inc. Corporation

# Chapter One

## ॐ

Quiet fell over the concert hall as the orchestra moved into the first notes of the closing composition. Perched on a stool in the center of the stage, the musician known simply as Devereaux calmly waited for his cue before launching into his signature piece, *Devereaux's Dance*. The guitar notes seemed to leap into the air, glittering and dancing as his fingers flew across the strings. When the last note shimmered across the hall, a deep moment of silence preceded a storm of applause. Devereaux bowed low, accepting the audience's acclaim, then strode from the stage, his mind already occupied with the next step in his plan.

In his dressing room, he quickly stripped off his formal clothing and stepped into the small shower stall. His friend and agent, Jake was waiting when he stepped back into the dressing room naked except for a small towel wrapped around his hips. Jake waggled one eyebrow in query. "No encore?"

When he shrugged in reply, the blue and green dragon tattoo that stretched across his left shoulder and biceps rippled. Jerking on the clothing laid out—gray silk boxers, soft faded jeans, plain navy blue t-shirt and polished black cowboy boots—Devereaux nodded once. "I'll give them one. Two minutes, Jake. After the encore, I'm out of here. No interviews. No autographs."

Jake soberly studied his friend and client. The hard, honed body usually camouflaged beneath a specially tailored tux was obvious in the soft comfortable jeans and shirt. Devereaux's golden hip-length hair, normally tucked out of sight beneath his jacket, slithered across his taut butt, confined in an elaborate French braid. "You're really coming out of the closet, Dev and going out there like that? Your fans don't know what a predator you really are."

"They'll get over it," Dev replied shortly while he shoved his wallet into his back pocket and slid a handful of change and his keys in his front pocket. "Next week, there will be a new sensation and they'll be saying 'Devereaux who?'"

Jake snorted in disgust. "Right! How many virtuoso musicians of your caliber play to sell out crowds? Violinists at your level are rare enough, but you play nearly every stringed instrument that exists! I'm not announcing your retirement. Go on this search you've planned. Find your damned mystery woman. When you get her out of your system, let me know and I'll arrange another tour." Shaking his head, he slammed out the door.

Dev surveyed the small room and pondered how anxious Jake would be to arrange another tour if he knew that it was just a cover for Dev's *day* job as an assassin. With the grim black humor he'd developed over the years, he decided that he should have acquired business cards with the legend "Troubleshooter for Hire". Maybe print it in blood red ink with a black rifle underscoring the title.

Once Jake was gone, Dev retrieved his personal weapons from their hiding places and swiftly distributed them about his person, before shrugging on his long black leather duster. He strapped on his chrome watch, slipped tiny gold hoops in his earlobes and slid his passport in his inside coat pocket. As a final touch, before leaving the dressing room, he put on his dark glasses and ducked to survey himself in the mirror. Not many dressing rooms were designed for someone over six four. Grinning, he shook his head, snagged his black cowboy hat and departed.

Stunned silence rippled across the auditorium as he strode confidently to the center of the stage with a sexy loose-hipped motion, took his violin and bow in hand and with no further ado, leaped into his most recent solo composition, never before performed in public. The reviewers the next day raved about the appropriately titled, *Dancer's Delight,* while avidly dissecting his changed appearance. What was not reported was the fact that Devereaux vanished when he walked off the stage after his final performance.

* * * * *

"He did what!" the angry voice exclaimed, echoing in the small conference room. Free Llewellyn had arctic blue eyes and a grim mouth. The tight lines radiating out from his flared nostrils declared that *someone* was going to pay for pissing him off in the very near future.

"He's dropped out of sight," Marcus replied calmly. The other men in the room had never seen Marcus in any mode other than calm and contained. Some speculated that it could be fatal to be around if he was in any other mode. After all, one did not get to be the commander of the Waterloo Group by being timid or squeamish—or hotheaded.

"Report," the Director demanded curtly.

"He left the stage after his main performance, changed to street clothes, returned to the stage and performed a totally new composition entitled *Dancer's Delight.* Then he exited the stage and no one's seen him since. No one saw him leave the building. No one recalls seeing him inside or outside. My office received a small package by messenger this morning. It was an envelope containing a business card with 'Assassin for Hire' printed on it with an anonymous phone number. Angelo checked it out. The card was self-printed on a standard ink-jet printer and when he called the phone number it rolled to a voice mail message that informed the caller that the individual was no longer accepting assignments as he had retired. The background music was *Dancer's Delight,*" Marcus added with sour humor. He shrugged. "Trackers couldn't find any trace of him. With the exception of the Traveller, he's the best we have. We won't find him until he wants us to, Mr. Llewellyn."

The Director stared at him for several long moments before reluctantly asking, "Where is the Traveller?"

"Asia...as far as we know. He hasn't been seen in the last week. If you're thinking that he'll help, you're dead wrong. You know they're a team." Tilting his head in thought, Marcus added, "The title of the encore and change from his normal cover was a deliberate gauntlet thrown down in public. He's challenging us to prevent him from retiring. And he's threatening us with substantial disclosure if we succeed."

"Find him. Neutralize him. And locate the Traveller," the Director said without inflection. "Make sure he's contained until you locate his brother."

"Dead or alive?" Marcus clarified fearlessly. It took brass balls to face down the relentlessly bitter old man who refused to retire, though retirement age was long past. There was considerable speculation that Marcus would take his place if he ever retired. More likely he would drop dead from sheer meanness. "You know the chance of bringing either of them in alive is slim to none."

"Do what you have to do." Passing sentence with no apparent remorse, the Director left the room without another word.

Less than a mile away Dancer Devereaux shopped at the local Wal-Mart in plain sight. Working from a short list compiled after much thought, he filled his cart with the items he expected he would need in coming days. He paused at a display of vegetable and flower seeds on clearance and rapidly picked through the packets, selecting them almost at random. Onions, potatoes, tomatoes, peppers, whatever herbs were left, marigolds, sunflowers and pumpkins and squash, although he had grave reservations about the squash. He found both regular corn and popcorn and several varieties of beans and broccoli. As an afterthought he strolled down to the book section and located a book on vegetable gardening basics and tossed it in the basket. Next, he strolled through the grocery aisles, tossing a bottle of peanut oil, a tiny bottle of candied ginger and a second tiny bottle of powdered curry into his basket, before randomly adding some bargain spices. Near the checkout area, he found a large battery display and tossed several packages into the basket as an afterthought. Finally, he checked out, selecting a long line and paid cash. Chucking his purchases into a battered gray Jeep he'd acquired in another name long ago, he sedately drove back to the studio apartment he'd rented at a transient hotel.

After preparing a quick meal of curried beef and broccoli, he ate while he checked his plans one last time. Finally, he packed everything tightly in a large tough leather backpack and set it by the door. Moving through the apartment, he meticulously erased every obvious trace of his presence while he reviewed his mental to-do list. It wouldn't pass muster if an actual forensics team was called in, but the point was not to trigger that happening. At last, satisfied that he had accomplished everything he had planned, he slipped on his jacket and gloves and hefting the backpack over one shoulder, left.

On the street, he turned down an alley, leisurely walked seven blocks until he reached a small garage, where he raised the broken door with a powerful heave revealing a small blue pickup, dented and pocked with rust. Tossing the pack on the ripped bench seat, he slid behind the wheel and located the keys tucked in the flap of the visor. Outward appearance to the contrary, it started on the first try and purred contentedly. He backed out, closed the garage door and drove away without a backward glance. His plans were set in motion. There was no going back. He would have to trust Trav to read the signs he'd left behind for him.

Twenty miles away, southeast of the city, he pulled into a shopping center and dropped an envelope containing the apartment keys in a mailbox. Nine hours away, north of the city, two states away, he pulled into a crowded, heavily wooded rest area, parking near the far end. After taking advantage of the facilities, he returned to the truck, slid the backpack over one shoulder and meandered down to the furthest picnic table. There, carefully observing his fellow travelers for nearly an hour, he rose at last and ghosted into the woods. Though the abandoned truck was noted within twenty-four hours, it wasn't connected to Dancer's disappearance until six weeks later. Time enough for him to reach his destination because Traveller did his part so well that they spent four weeks searching for them in the Southwest desert.

# Chapter Two

## ❧

Oppressive heat blanketed Mystic Valley just after noon. In the deep shade of the large potting shed on the edge of the communal garden, Eppie pored over her notes in disgust. There was absolutely no reason for the experimental failure, but the *foltins* and *drackas* she was trying to cultivate simply did not survive. Tossing her stylus down on the grubby sheets of crumpled *linual*, she sighed before shoving the tiny pots to the side of the rough table. She longed for a real building—not a simple shed—with ample space for her experiments and notes, but it seemed that no one really took her interest in plants seriously. After all she was a *woman*, expected to bond eventually and have babies. Even her mother, Jade—who should have understood—didn't seem to understand how important her plant work was to her.

She looked up when a shadowy presence suddenly blocked the doorway, surprised when she recognized her petite sister. "Wrenna! What are you doing out breaking the nooning rest?"

"Delivering more of those small pots," Wrenna replied cheerfully. "Where do you want them?"

Eppie wiped her brow with the back of her hand and pointed to a stand in the corner. "Over there, I guess. Why didn't you get one of the boys to carry them for you? Couldn't that wait until later when it is cooler?"

"Well, I suppose so, but Llyon was anxious to know how your experiments with the *foltins* and *drackas* came out. Since I had to deliver the pots anyway, I told him I would ask." Wrenna sat down on the bench beside the door and cocked a curious eyebrow at her oldest sister. "And why should I ask one of the boys to carry them out, when I'm perfectly capable of doing it myself? Any luck?"

Sighing in discouragement, Eppie shook her head. "No. I wish I could determine what the secret is. Or failing that, I wish the next person to enter the valley would bring potato and onion seeds. That's what Mama said they're called out-valley. I've tried everything I can think of and nothing works. They refuse to grow as cultivated vegetables." She slumped back on her high stool in frustration. "Tell Llyon that he's going to have to forage for the wild ones this season if he wants them for dinner."

"Hah! You think he has time for foraging?" Wrenna winced when she snagged some of her bright red hair on the rough siding of the shed. Gently working the fine strands free, she smoothed them back in place, tucking the loose strands beneath her tightly braided knot high on her head. "He's busy riding herd on the younglings."

"Where are Mama and Papa?" Eppie asked in a dangerously quiet tone.

"Hmmm. Let's see. Papa walked down to Bell's Corners. It's his clinic day. And Mama and the math twins are working on some new problem. Some new idea they have about the caves and portals. You know what that means…"

"I know—we won't see them until they come up for air in a couple of weeks." Her gaze narrowed as she stared at the garden thoughtfully. "When do they plan for Llyon to finish his healer's apprenticeship? Healing isn't exactly something that he can learn by osmosis." Turning back to her samples, she studied them with annoyance. "I may as well clean up here. If I take over kitchen duty, Llyon can study this afternoon. Tell him I'll be in shortly."

"Dinner is already done," Wrenna told her, a small smile tugging at her mouth. "You know Ly—he always plans well ahead. Anyway, he's talking to Arano and Tyger in the kitchen. You should come in because Arano told us that your mystery man is coming soon."

Eppie whipped around to face her sister, nearly tipping her stool. "What? When?"

Wrenna shrugged, brushed away the faint sheen of moisture on her forehead and shot Eppie a teasing grin as she stood up. "Soon?" she answered and retreated at an unseemly trot.

Hurriedly gathering her notes in an untidy bundle, Eppie stuffed them in the deep pocket of the dirt-smeared tan smock covering her pale green *meerlim* as she picked her way through the garden to the low gate opening out on the main path. The filmy cap perched over her dark hair threatened to slide down over her ear, but she daren't touch it with her muddy hands. She sighed again. No doubt old Marta would be peeking out her window and note Eppie's shortcomings, but that was always the way it was. By the time she had walked three houses down to her parents' home, her steps slowed as she calmed down, considering the possible meanings behind Arano's prediction.

She sat down on the smooth stone front steps beneath the shade of the wide porch and worked to clear her mind. Once she was ready, she closed her eyes and sent out a mental tendril. *Dancer?*

*Here,* he acknowledged immediately on a somewhat grim note. *How did you know I was on the mountain?*

*Guessed. I was hoping you were near,* she pointed out gently. *Are you well? You feel angry and tired...and sad?*

There was a closed-off mental silence for several moments and then, *I suppose all of those things are true,* he admitted reluctantly. *I'm hiking up the main face of Bright Shadows Mountain. Not too far behind me is a team assigned to capture or kill me. I need to reach my hideout without being observed. And to make life complete, the weather is getting very cold and nasty.* She felt his wry flash of amusement. *So! How's your day been?*

*Up to this point, not nearly as exciting as yours,* she replied readily. *But any day I can speak to you is a good day. I wish I knew a way to help you.*

*Well, since we've never figured out how to meet, we'll just have to put that on hold for now. I need to concentrate on my back trail, so I'll get back to you later.*

*Be careful,* she sent softly, brushing his mind gently once more before breaking their connection. As she sat there, the familiar clenching wave of *schalzina* rolled through her belly, causing her womb to contract and a gush of silky fluid to drench her swollen labia. She wrapped her arms across her belly and bent over, willing the wave to recede. As it faded away, she breathed a sigh of relief, though she admitted that her time was short. If Dancer didn't arrive soon and join her in the oath-binding before she entered the final stages of *schalzina,* she would die. She wanted to deny that possibility, but each time was worse.

The door opened and closed softly and a long male body slumped down on the steps next to her. She shot her younger brother a swift questioning glance before turning back to stare down at her bare toes. "What's wrong, Wolfe?"

His dark eyes flashed with anger. "Too much testosterone in the kitchen," he replied shortly. "I had to get out of there before I bashed their heads together."

"I don't suppose you're talking about Arano, so it must be Llyon and Tyger?"

"Of course. Who else makes us all crazy?" He rose and paced out to the path and back. "Why can they not see they need to be together?" he demanded angrily.

"You know this is something they must work out," she replied softly. "Mama says they will when they're ready. A covenant bond for siblings is something that's only sanctioned every two or three centuries. Their twin-bond is difficult enough to deal with." She sat waiting for his to calm down. When he plopped down next to her and groaned, she laughed.

He shook his head and the jeweled *chinkas* binding his twenty-five dark braids tinkled musically. She leaned against him, nudging his shoulder. "Concentrate on your own mate, brother."

He snorted and nudged her back. "My mate is more unattainable than yours. We're an odd pair, Eppie."

"We're all strange," she countered. "It must be the valley mixing with the out-valley. Even Dai can't quite decide what's happening with us. Personally, I almost think that's the strangest part of it. Papa and Dai are scratching their heads over the weird things that are happening. No one can really predict how things will come out." She brushed his hand gently. "I suppose I better go in, get cleaned up and see what Arano has to say."

He stood and pulled her to her feet. "I think I'll go for a walk down to the river. I wish you joy if what Arano says is true. I know you've waited a long time for your man."

After several moments of deep calming breaths, she went in, washed her hands thoroughly and straightened her small filmy cap. Knowing just how perceptive Llyon was, she lightly pinched her cheeks and relaxed the tense muscles in her belly and back before joining her siblings in the old comforting kitchen.

When she entered, Arano was obviously waiting for her. He leaned on the counter next to Llyon, sipping from his mug of chamomile tea. Wondering what Dancer would think of her brothers, she looked at them with fresh eyes. Llyon and his twin, Tyger towered over her, large young men with the hard muscles developed from manual labor and their warrior training. Their fiery red hair was confined in the prescribed twenty-five braids of the warriors, secured with their personal *chinkas*. Though bare-chested because of the heat, their silky kilt-like *shardas* clung to firm sweaty flanks and muscular legs, revealing more than they concealed. Sandals with laces that twined up their calves to secure their flicknife sheaths completed their ensembles.

21

Except for his shiny black hair, Arano was a mirror copy of his elder brothers. They all shared the same tilted black eyes, glittering with repressed humor, delicately pointed ears, smooth blue tinged skin and elongated eyeteeth. Papa had once tried to explain that out-valley people were different and when they encountered the valley people, they usually thought they were elves or vampires. From his tone, his children concluded that an elf or vampire wasn't necessarily a good thing in the eyes of the out-valley.

Arano handed his empty mug to Tyger and cocked an eyebrow in query. "You've talked to your man?"

"Yes," she admitted calmly. "A group is pursuing him — he said to capture or kill him."

"He will find his way here tomorrow or the next day, I think. Soon…" Arano said thoughtfully. Tapping his chin with one long finger, he shook his head slowly. "I cannot see if his pursuers will follow him, but I see *him* in the valley." He flashed her a brief grin. "Very attractive, too."

"We're always prepared for intruders, if necessary," Tyger reminded them. "Of course, it would be better if he managed to arrive alone."

"True. However, we must deal with the real possibility of others following him. So, I suggest that you make what preparations you need to deal with that eventuality." Having delivered his message, Arano abruptly left, allowing the kitchen door to slam behind him.

Llyon silently stirred the *rowan* stew in the huge pot on the stove, before inhaling deeply. "Sit down, Eppie. You need the rest. Tyger, get her a mug of *wachaz* tea," he directed as he placed a small pot of honey on the table.

"*Wachaz* tea?" Wrenna queried as she walked through the door. "Who needs *wachaz* tea?"

"Eppie. She's begun *schalzina* and the tea will calm the contractions," Llyon replied while coolly checking Eppie's pulse. "What?" he asked when he saw the irritated expression on her face. "You thought I wouldn't know? What kind of healer would I be?"

"I could wish, just once in a while that there was some privacy in this household," Eppie said tartly. "It's annoying when everyone knows your personal business."

Tyger bit his lip to keep from laughing before inquiring, "And exactly why would you be any different from any other member of this household? With fourteen of us here, you're lucky you get to use the bathing room alone. Be happy you have to sit down to pee." He tossed one of the tiny prepared gauze bags of *wachaz* leaves into a deep red mug, poured boiling water over it and set the mug in front of Eppie. "How long has this been going on?" he asked seriously.

"Two—no, three years," she answered casually.

The silence in the kitchen was deafening. Then a deep voice observed from the doorway, "Well, it would appear that your man will get here just in time. What do you plan to do? Meet him at the cave, drag him out to the circle and demand that he bond with you immediately?" her Papa inquired with faint sarcasm.

Eppie gnawed on her lips. "Not exactly…"

"So what is the plan?" Tyger asked, absently reaching out to pick at the tray of golden sweet pies.

Llyon rapped his twin's knuckles with his wooden spoon. "Don't touch!" Shifting the pies away from temptation's reach, he snatched up a pile of pale green pottery bowls and handed them to Ty. "Set the table, please."

"Sure." Swiftly dealing out the bowls like a deck of cards, he pursued his own line of thought. "How are you going to explain bonding to him, Eppie?"

"Carefully," she muttered before burying her nose in her mug. Everything was everybody's business. She longed for a place where no one wanted to know anything about her. "Very carefully," she repeated.

Wrenna got up and gathered utensils and heavy cloth napkins. In an effort to deflect the discussion away from Eppie, she poked Tyger in the chest and demanded, "So, when are *you* going to settle down?"

Again a frozen silence settled over the kitchen. Llyon, facing the stove, held himself still with an effort that left him trembling. Ty propped his long body against the heavy wooden dish cabinet, carefully settling his healing ankle on a low stool and thoughtfully stared at his twin's rigid back. "When my bond mate is ready," he answered evenly, "I will be happy to settle down. In the meantime, you are old enough to find your own bond mate. After all, you don't want to just be a potter your whole life, do you?"

"And why not? Don't you plan to be a weaver for the rest of your life? Should it be any different because I'm a female?" Wrenna tossed napkins and utensils on the table and stalked out of the room.

Merlyn, their father, surveyed them all in silence. Then, in a tone that brooked no defiance, he observed, "This discussion is closed. Eppie, after dinner, I recommend a hot soak in the tub before you go home. Tyger and Llyon will walk you home when you're ready."

Llyon frowned. "Ty's ankle is hurting. I can walk her home alone."

"Broken ankles take a long time to heal. Ty needs to exercise it to strengthen it. Walk slowly. Besides, walking Eppie home will get you both out of the house until the younglings are settled down." Merlyn's tone clearly conveyed his wishes would be carried out.

With a shrug, Llyon laughed and surrendered to the inevitable. "At least the dishes will be done by the time we get back."

"Everything for dinner is prepared?" Merlyn confirmed quietly. Llyon nodded. "Then I strongly suggest that the two of you find someplace else to be. I wish to talk to Eppie alone."

Without comment, the twins went out the back door, leaving Merlyn and Eppie in blessed quiet. "Have you talked to your young man about bonding, Eppie?"

She flinched, wishing she wasn't having this conversation right now. "A little. I've mentioned generalities, but not specifics," she admitted finally.

"Just how general?" he inquired mildly. "Bonding is pretty damned specific."

"Well-ll, I mentioned that it's a lifelong commitment. And I told him about part of the oath-binding ceremony..."

"Which part?" he asked without looking at her.

She hated when he asked her stuff and refused to look at her. It always made her feel like she was a toddling youngling. She sipped her tea as she marshaled her thoughts. "We don't talk about this kind of stuff very often," she confessed. "Usually, we just talk about things we find interesting—"

"And bonding with your mate isn't one of the things you find interesting?"

"I didn't say that. It's just not something that came up in conversation—"

"Don't you think it should?" He did look at her then. "Eppie, you're my oldest child. I've had you around for the longest and I have a special place in my heart for you. I want you to be happy and I know that for you, perhaps more than any other child of mine, that happiness will rest on the relationship you have with your bond mate." He sighed. "This man will arrive here most likely disoriented, confused and stressed. When your Mama and I arrived here before you were born, it was difficult for us and we had each other to depend on. Dancer is alone and running for his life. I remember what that was like. If I'm reading the signs correctly, you have very little time until you must bond or risk your losing your life. Yes?"

"Yes."

"Then if it were me, I would start a dialogue very quickly about your needs and expectations with this man. I seriously doubt that he's going to be enthusiastic about jumping into a bonding immediately upon his arrival," he pointed out with a faint hint of humor. "I don't see the bedding part as a problem, but the commitment of the oath-binding requires some thought and consideration. The more time he has to think about it, the better."

Eppie hunched her shoulders and sighed. "I know, Papa. I just haven't figured out how to approach it. It's hard to just start talking about something so personal."

"Eppie." Merlyn's gentle, tender tone nearly brought her to tears. "If you truly have an attachment with him, your entire relationship is *personal*. Attachment and bonding don't leave room for anything else. Talk to him." He got to his feet, leaned over to softly kiss her forehead and left the room without another word.

She gathered their mugs and carried them to the sink before leaving the house. On the path, she stood a moment, undecided about her destination, then abruptly headed down to the river path toward the lake. There was a quiet spot with a bench facing the river and she needed a few private moments to think before she talked to Dancer again.

# Chapter Three

ॐ

Gauzy trailing scarves of mist veiled the peaks of Bright Shadows Mountain and its hanging valleys with their honeycomb of caves. Intermittent blasts of sleet blurred the sloping cracked slabs thrust up by the ancient clashing of Mother Earth's tectonic plates. Dancer paused for a moment to stare at the tumble of broken boulders and split granite megaliths surrounding him. Then climbing steadily, carefully picking his way along a pebble-strewn trail, he nimbly avoided the slow trickles of water that were gradually swelling to bubbling streams.

As he moved upward through shifting walls of gray, invisible squirrels chattered at him, icy water dripped ceaselessly from the trees, and leaves and pine needles pelted him from above. Driven by gusting winds, heaving mountain laurel slapped him in the face and caught at his hair, snagging fine golden brown strands from their confining braid. Impatiently, he brushed the wet, irritating wisps back from his damp face. Reaching a point with a clear view of his back trail, he paused to check on the progress of his pursuers and noted that they were gaining just a bit. *Not good.* Abruptly, he left the trail, plunging up a stony creek bed.

A rush of icy water flooded the creek, tumbling rocks and debris in his path. The cold water seeped through the seams of his hiking boots, chilling his feet. His soaked jeans and jacket clung to his clammy skin, chafing the tender skin of his inner thighs and underarms. He shifted his heavy leather backpack to a more comfortable spot, miserably shivering from the deepening cold and smarting from the irritation to his hide. Taking another sudden change in direction, he scrambled up over a field of boulders, wove through a small stand of pines and then stepped into another bubbling brook, slogging down through a tiny narrow canyon. Just as he stepped from the brook onto a flat slab of rock, the sleet changed to driving wet snow.

With satisfaction, knowing the snow would blot out his trail, he stepped into the shadow of a towering rock spire and minutely searched his back trail until he was completely positive he was alone. Then, shrugging off his backpack, he wormed his way through the dark, narrow descending passage behind the spire, backpack in one hand and his flashlight in the other. The passage, though short, was claustrophobic in proportions and he was thankful to reach the end where it opened into a spacious, dry cave.

After a quick flash around to confirm that it was empty, he gently set down the backpack and shrugged out of his wet coat. Gathering materials from the well-stocked woodpile, he quickly built a fire in the stone fire circle, shivering all the while in the cool, dry air. Once he was confident that the fire was burning brightly, he dragged his pack closer and set about changing into warmer dry clothing. By the time he was finished, he was so exhausted he had to push himself to heat enough water to fill his thermos for hot tea while he munched on a crunchy food bar.

After gulping down the hot tea as fast as he could without burning his mouth, he shook out the bedding on the rough bunk he'd constructed over the past few visits, spread his sleeping bag on top and tumbled into bed, slipping off the edge of consciousness.

A faint lull in the storm dragged him back to reluctant awareness. Prying one eye open, he saw that his fire had burned down to dim coals. He sat up, every joint creaking, heaved a deep sigh and slowly stood up, fumbling on his moccasins. Limping over to his fire pit, he squatted down and rebuilt his fire. The tone of the storm had changed. Wriggling back up the cramped passage, he peeked out across the canyon, astonished at the deep drifts of snow that filled the narrow canyon floor.

With a sly smile, he reflected on the fortunes of his pursuers, caught in a blinding blizzard on the mountain. Things were looking up. With a happier outlook, he returned to his shelter, found his bottle of Aleve and swallowed two tablets with the lukewarm tea left in his thermos. Then, wearily, he returned to his bed, scrunching around until he was enclosed in his warm sleeping bag and drifted back to sleep.

Deep in the wee hours of the morning he woke abruptly, heart pounding. Keeping as still as possible, he tried to discern what had tripped his internal alarm. Then he caught a whiff of lilacs and roses and froze. After a moment, he clambered to his feet and cautiously limped back up the tight tunnel to the canyon. More snow. Deep piles of howling, wind-driven snow, but for sure, no lilacs or roses. Returning to his shelter, he searched the cave interior, but the scent had faded away, leaving a bare hint in the air. He rebuilt his fire and prepared a peanut butter and banana sandwich while he heated some water for tea. With regret, he peeled his last banana, knowing that it might be a while before he had another.

*Dancer? Are you awake?*

*I'm awake,* he admitted with a hint of humor. *A really offbeat odor in the air woke me out of a dead sleep.*

*What was it?* Eppie demanded with anticipation. Papa and Mama had commented about smelling flowers right before they found their way to the valley.

*You'll probably think I'm crazy, but I thought I smelled lilacs and roses.* She could almost see the smile in his tone. *I made it safely to that cave I told you about and I'm nearly positive that I wasn't followed. There's about two feet of snow on the ground outside, so I figure the guys behind me are probably holed up wherever they were able to find shelter. No way I should smell flowers in this weather.*

*Are you sure it wasn't a dream?* she teased gently.

*No, it wasn't a dream,* he assured her. *The scent was still there after I got up to investigate. Why are you awake?*

*I've been sitting here in front of my fire, thinking. I have something I need to talk to you about and I've been trying to decide how to explain things.* He could sense her nervousness and anxiety. *It's a little awkward,* she warned him.

*In my experience, the more awkward it is, the better it is to just say it and get it off your chest. Once it's out, we can deal with it.*

*Well, don't say I didn't warn you first.* He could almost see her taking a deep breath before she plunged in, *You know I've told you something about our bonding customs here in the valley? How we bond for life?*

*Yes, I remember. You bond for life and sex is impossible with anyone except your bond mate. What's wrong? You been hiding a bond mate from me?*

*I can't do that because* you're *my bond mate.*

For a brief startled moment, he wondered if he had misunderstood, but almost immediately, he rejected that thought. *Eppie,* he pointed out gently, *I can't be your bond mate if I'm not in the valley.*

She sighed in frustration. *I am quite aware that you're not in the valley,* she replied tartly. *But you will be here soon. When you get here, we need to bond as soon as you arrive. Without the formal bonding, I will die,* she finished with a rush.

*Whoa! Wait a minute! What is this stuff about dying? What the hell are you talking about?* he demanded. *And why would you think I'm coming to the valley?* He sat on his bunk and held his head in his hands. Suddenly, he had a raging headache. What in the world had he gotten involved in? She was just a nice woman he talked to in his mind. He had no idea how old she was—she could be anywhere from twelve to ninety—though he suspected she was close to his own age.

*My brother, Arano, sees things. He says he has seen you here in the next few days. You said you smelled the roses and lilacs just like my parents did before they came.* Her very reasonable tone as though she was talking to a three-year-old irked him. *If we had not formed a formal attachment, we wouldn't be able to talk to each other.*

He stood and went to his backpack, rummaging for his Aleve even as he admitted it wasn't going to be strong enough to deal with the migraine he felt building. Fighting to hold on to his temper, he replied as evenly as possible. *I have enjoyed our conversations, but that doesn't mean I want to take the relationship any further. You seem like a nice woman, Eppie, but I don't really know you and I have absolutely no desire to bond with you – or anyone else at this time. Right now I just want a quiet place where I can cook and write music.*

Immediately, she shut him out and slumped in her chair, devastated at his unexpected rejection. Curling up like a *pilkie* bug, she rocked against the soft chair back, too desolated even for tears. Never in her worst dreams had she anticipated his reaction.

Back at Lost Market Tyger woke to the soft sounds of Llyon dressing. "What's wrong? Don't you know it's the middle of the night?" he demanded grumpily.

Grimly, Llyon retorted, "Open your shields and you'll know why I'm getting dressed."

Because of his calling as a healer Llyon had long ago learned to partially shield his mind against intrusion while allowing him a certain awareness of those around him. Tyger, as a weaver, had no such need and had never bothered to learn to partially shield. When he let down his shields the wall of grief emanating from Eppie nearly flattened him. He slammed up his shields, leaped from bed and hastily dressed in *sharda* and sandals, lacing them with the speed of long practice. Following Llyon's example, he twisted his hair up in a tangled knot anchored with two long slender picks as he limped down the hall after his twin.

Merlyn met them at the front door, knotting up his own tangled locks. "What the hell happened?" he demanded as

Llyon opened the door. "I can't tell anything except that she's hurting."

"I don't know for sure Papa, but I think it has something to do with her man. What did you two talk about this afternoon?"

"I told her she had to discuss bonding with him before he got here," Merlyn explained in bafflement. "What could have happened?"

Tyger led the way down the dark path. "Probably, he told her he wasn't interested. After all, based on things you and Mama have explained about the out-valley, his perceptions of their relationship are probably very different from hers." The circle of light from his lightstone bobbed wildly as he gestured to emphasize his point. "It will all depend on what she said."

Llyon brushed past Tyger and led the way across the clearing to Eppie's cabin. Shoving the door open without the courtesy of a cursory knock, he swept the cabin with a quick glance, settling on her form curled up in the chair by her fire. Seconds later, he pulled her into his arms, offering what comfort he could, while rapidly assessing her physical condition. With relief, he sensed that physically she was well, even if she was emotionally wrecked. The absence of tears worried him, but when Merlyn and Tyger joined them, she abruptly started weeping. Easing her into Merlyn's embrace, he and Tyger moved back, allowing them some privacy. A rapid check of the cabin assured them that she was alone and they went outside to check the perimeter of the clearing.

While they were gone, Merlyn coaxed her into giving him a brief explanation of her conversation with Dancer. "Well," he conceded quietly, "I was thinking of a less abrupt approach. I reckon you'll have to give him a little while to digest what you said."

"How can you say that? It's hard to misunderstand when someone says they're not interested!" She sat up, scrubbing at her face and glared at her Papa. "It was your idea to talk to him."

"And you promptly told him he had to bond with you or you would die," he retorted with grim humor. "No out-valley guy would see that as anything other than emotional blackmail. Then, according to what you just told me, you compounded it by offering no additional details. Small wonder that he said 'thanks, but no thanks'." He went into her tiny bathing room, found a small bathing cloth, dampened it with warm water and brought it back to her. Tilting her head back with one hand, he wiped her face carefully. "I suggest that you put this entire thing aside until he arrives in the valley. At that point, you can expand your explanations as necessary. Until then, it's all moot."

"I suppose you think I'm silly…"

"No. Just overtired. Get in bed. I'll send Llyon in to put you to sleep. Tomorrow morning things will look better." Kissing her gently on her forehead, he gave her a gentle shove toward her bed and went outside to locate Llyon.

The twins sat on the porch steps talking quietly. Llyon looked up at their father and inquired, "How is she?"

"She's been better, but I think a good night's sleep will help. Can you just go give her a nudge? Otherwise, she'll just lie there, worrying the rest of the night."

Llyon promptly stood, shook his *sharda* into place and went inside. Moments later, he reappeared, silently pulling the door closed. "She'll sleep the rest of the night," he muttered softly. "Do you want me to stay here with her?"

"No…" Merlyn tilted his head in thought. "I think she'll need to be alone in the morning. Let's go home."

\* \* \* \* \*

In his cave, Dancer sat considering his odd conversation with Eppie. What exactly did she mean when she claimed she would die if they didn't bond? Was it some weird type of feminine exaggeration? What if it was the literal truth? How could that be? She seemed thoroughly convinced that he would be arriving in her hidden valley very soon. What was it she said about her parents smelling flowers right before they arrived there? Was it some kind of strange drug or hallucination?

He shrugged in bewilderment, deciding that he didn't have enough pieces to really make sense of the puzzle and went to make himself some tea. What was this attachment she mentioned? He had the odd notion she pronounced it like it should be italics. *Attachment.* As if it was something extra special. With shame he reluctantly admitted that sophistication wasn't the first word that came to mind when describing her and he wondered if he had led her to believe there was more to their relationship than an innocent flirtation. After a while, finished with his tea, he shrugged again and crawled back into bed. Tomorrow was another day and he had much to do. On that optimistic note, he fell asleep.

# Chapter Four

ຂາ

The next day Dancer waited in vain for Eppie to get in touch with him as he puttered around, arranging things so he would be comfortable while he waited for Traveller to arrive. He finished building a rough table and a stool he'd started on a previous visit. He checked the canyon twice and both times marveled that the storm still raged, piling more snow in towering drifts. He dug out a field latrine in a tiny alcove that was a small extension in one back corner of his cave and then as an afterthought, he screened it off for privacy. While building the screen, he pondered the odd human need for privacy, even when alone.

When evening approached and she still hadn't made any attempt to break her silence, he made his own effort to reach Eppie and met a solid blank wall. As he worked, it occurred to him just how comfortable he was communicating with her mind to mind. Unexpectedly, the cold silence between them disturbed him. He couldn't pinpoint a precise time, but somewhere along the line, he had become accustomed to her nebulous presence with him and now he missed her more than he expected. And then he told himself he was acting like a lovelorn teenager and with stubborn determination he set their conversation aside. After fixing himself another sandwich for his evening meal, he did a sketchy body wash and tumbled into bed, hoping for an uninterrupted night of sleep.

In the dark cold hour before dawn, he woke, alert and alarmed. Though there was no hint of light from the outside, here deep in his cave, he knew without checking his watch that it was close to five o'clock in the morning. The scent of roses and lilacs was heavy in the closed-in space. Moving as little as possible, he minutely examined the cave from his warm cocoon of blankets. There was no one there. Nothing was out of place. Reluctantly easing from bed, he slipped on his moccasins and made the trek to the entrance. The storm was winding down, but no one was going to be traveling through the canyon for a while.

When he returned to the warm comfort of his cave, the scent struck him with a heavy blow. Where the hell was it coming from?

Starting just to the right of his entry way, he carefully examined the cave walls, looking for cracks and fissures where the floral vapors could seep into the cave. Just past his latrine alcove, he discovered a wide opening hidden by an overlapping wall of stone. A draft of warm air, laden with the powerful scent of flowers washed around him. With shock, he stood motionless, staring at the optical illusion, wanting to deny that he could possibly have missed it in all of the visits he had made to the cave. He spread his arms, guesstimating a rough measurement of three feet for the width of the passage and shook his head in sharp denial. No way had he missed an opening that size. Going back to his pack, he retrieved his heavy-duty flashlight and started to explore the strange corridor when a sudden thought had him pausing.

*What if this was the way into the valley? What if he couldn't return?*

Abruptly, he turned away and began to straighten his belongings in the cave. He washed and dressed in clean clothing, ran a brush through his hair and rapidly braided it and did a quick pass with his toothbrush. When all was in order, he scribbled a note to Traveller and left it propped against a pile of books on the table. Then he repacked his backpack and shouldered it on, folding his coat and stuffing it between the straps. Finally, he turned his oil lamps out, covered the small fire with dirt and then made his way to the tunnel. Flashlight flickering into the smothering darkness ahead of him, he began his exploration.

The corridor was fairly short, but quite twisty. When he reached the end, it opened into another small cave. Across the room, the roar of a waterfall masked all possible sound. He stood in the entrance, studying his surroundings carefully. Retreating about halfway back in the tunnel, he set his pack down before returning to the new cavern. His deliberate decision to leave his pack in the passage was a feeble attempt to keep the tunnel open while he explored. He had no idea if it would accomplish what he wanted or not.

Crossing the cave to the waterfall, he saw that a path led to the outside from behind the waterfall and after mentally tossing a coin, he followed the path from the cave. It led to a small grassy lawn approximately ten feet across with a stone bench situated next to the pool the waterfall plunged into. The pool was small—he judged it was less than six feet across—and had a rocky, shallow overflow creek leading away into the surrounding woods. When he looked up, he saw that the waterfall apparently sprang from nowhere, straight out from halfway up a sheer cliff wall that towered above the cave for at least thirty feet. *Weird.*

He prowled across the lawn, between two huge stone sentinels and found himself in a stone circle, complete with an enormous flat stone altar in the center. The tiny hairs on the back of his neck stood up in visceral alarm as he took in the full picture. Every stone was elaborately carved with spirals and other ancient symbols. A line of distinct glyphs spiraled around each stone from top to bottom. The alter stone had a row of glyphs around the sides just below the flat top. Then below them, there were more spirals and spiky sun signs and checkerboard patterns of lines. *Well, now.*

He inched back out of the circle very slowly, then turned and ran back to the cave, unashamed of his fear. Somewhere in his brief flight, he decided he'd explored all he cared to and he would return to his own cave. He hustled behind the waterfall, stumbling to a halt when he saw his pack sitting squarely in the center of the small cave. His eyes flew to the space where the tunnel entrance had been, but solid rock wall filled the area now. His legs went rubbery with shock and he sat down with an abruptness that was going to leave him with bruises for a while. With a peculiar, sour smile, he concluded that ready or not, he had arrived in Eppie's valley.

* * * * *

After their aborted conversation, Eppie had spent the previous day cleaning her cabin, doing laundry and mulling over her options. There weren't many, she admitted. She had clearly botched her conversation with Dancer and she was just cowardly enough that she wasn't ready to attempt another explanation just yet. Papa had made his own views quite plain. It was up to her to correct their misunderstanding.

By evening, she was tired of her own company and quite happy when her mama arrived in company with Wrenna. There were very few limits in Jade's life due to her blindness, but walking around in the valley alone was one of them. Fortunately, with fourteen children, there was usually someone available and willing to act as a guide. While the ladies settled themselves at the table, Eppie prepared *quoltania* tea and set out some sweet lavender wafers. "I'm happy to see you, Mama, but what has you venturing out here?"

Jade smiled and teased, "Are you accusing me of being nosy?"

"Of course not, but you have to admit that you don't often visit me here. Did Papa send you as reinforcements?" Eppie set the mugs on the table and absently placed her mama's fingers on the handle. "Honey?"

"Please." Jade gently stirred the tea, before taking a cautious sip. "I thought perhaps you could use a woman's perspective. Much as I love your papa, he's a *man,* with a man's strange take on things. Will you tell me about it?"

Eppie sighed and sat down with an ungraceful thump. "Mama, I almost don't know where to begin. We've talked about all sorts of things...now suddenly he tells me I'm a nice woman, but he's not interested?" She looked at her mama, as always surprised at her eternally youthful appearance. No one looking at her deep auburn hair and clear turquoise eyes and unwrinkled skin would guess that she had borne so many children.

Wrenna snorted. "At least he thinks you're nice."

Shaking her head, Jade clarified, "Nice is a word out-valley men use when they want to give you the brush-off."

"Is that what it sounds like?" Wrenna demanded in disgust.

"Exactly. So if he tells her she's nice, it's his way of backing off. However, I assume that you've been letting him stew in his own juices?" Jade inquired mildly.

"Mama," Eppie protested with a laugh, "you have a very colorful way with words. I just couldn't talk to him after that. I warned him that the subject was awkward and he assured me that we would work it out. Then, he got upset and told me he didn't want to bond with *anyone*." She twisted her mug in her hands and fought for a way to explain her churning feelings. "It was his tone. He was sort of curt and short...and appalled."

"And? Weren't you also blunt? Bond with me or I die?" Jade sat back and folded her hands together, rubbing her thumbs together. "Take time tonight to really look at it from his viewpoint. He knows absolutely nothing about us and our physical needs. Valley men and out-valley men are much the same. A hard cock and full balls and they're ready to function," she said with calm bluntness. "Women out-valley are somewhat similar. Attraction to any man is really all they need to function. Their body prepares them for sex. But valley women are distinctly different. Without *attachment* or formal bonding, we don't feel any sexual urges or attraction. And once one or the other is present, we no longer have control over the physical changes. That's why the women in the valley choose the bond mates. He needs to understand the difference."

"How is she supposed to explain it if out-valley women are so different?" Wrenna asked with intent curiosity. "Is it really true they have sex with any man they want?"

"She should tell him exactly what I just said," Jade replied. "And yes, they are capable of having sex with multiple partners, though they may choose not to. Why are you so interested, Wrenna?"

"Curiosity," Wrenna hedged.

"No, I don't think so. There's something more…"

Feeling harassed and pressured, Wrenna blurted out, "Well, if you must know, it's because I'm pretty sure my mate is also an out-valley man." Clapping her hands over her mouth, she stared at Eppie in horror.

"Real-ly." Jade tilted her head to one side, almost as though she could see Wrenna's face and said, "Well, pay attention. Maybe you can learn something from Eppie's experience." She pushed back from the table and stood. "I think we've said enough for now. Come, Wrenna. It's time for us to go home. You can tell me about your man on the way." Wrenna hastily gulped down her tea and followed her mama out the door, leaving Eppie to her contemplations in lonely silence. In a little while, with no useful conclusions, Eppie twisted off her lightstones and went off to bed.

In the clear light of early morning, Eppie woke to the sound of birds twittering their morning songs. She slowly stretched and turned over to look out into her small garden. Bumblebees blundered among her hollyhocks while the busy honeybees droned in the flowering herbs. Colorful butterflies flittered from the clumps of asters and zinnias to the flourishing bed of sweet peas and cosmos. Her bee balm had a mix of bees and butterflies vying for the best blooms. As always, just watching the action soothed her in a way that nothing else did. The bright gold and orange faces of her sunflowers cheered her up.

As she lay there, yawning, she couldn't think of one single reason to get up early. The communal garden wasn't in need of her attention. Her experiments had failed again and she wasn't in the mood to make another attempt just yet. Perhaps she would stay home today and work in her own garden. The beans and tomatoes needed to be staked. And the grass around the walkway was ready for a trim. A jaw-cracking yawn caught her by surprise, bringing tears to her eyes. With a sigh, she rolled out of bed and headed for her bathing room, reflecting that she was going to have to bribe the twins into installing a tub for her because there were days that a shower just didn't pass muster.

After dressing and bolting down toasted bread slathered with *quoltania* jam, orange *rowan* cheese and hot tea, she took her second mug with her and went to sit on her front steps. She had put off her responsibilities long enough. It was time to talk to Dancer. Ready or not.

*Dancer? Are you awake?*

*You could say that,* he replied curtly. *Thanks to you, I'm pretty sure I'm stuck in your valley. You and your disappearing tunnels and flower smells —*

*Where are you?* she interrupted boldly. *What happened?*

*I woke up this morning with the smell of flowers again. When I started investigating the source, I found an odd tunnel and explored it. Now the tunnel's gone and I'm sitting in a little cave with a waterfall across the entrance. There's some weird stone circle outside,* he added in an aggrieved tone.

Though very tempted to laugh, she prudently refrained because something told her that he wasn't finding his experience amusing in any respect. After a brief moment of consideration, she observed, *You're in one of the pledging circles. There are several of them spread across the valley. I need you to go back to the circle and look at the symbols on the central stone.*

*For what?* his disgruntled tone made it clear that he wasn't anxious to return to the circle, but she needed the information only he could provide.

Trying to project soothing calm, she explained, *Look at the stone and tell me how many spirals are in each sequence of symbols.*

There was a lot of low muttering in the back of her mind, but she took care not to listen too closely to what she suspected was a lot of colorful cursing. After a few moments, he informed her, *Three spirals between each set of symbols. Do you know where I am now?*

*I know exactly where you are,* she assured him. *My cabin is nearby, so I should be there shortly. If you'll be more comfortable, wait for me next to the pool.*

*I have a strong feeling that* nothing *is going to make me comfortable for a long while.*

*Well, that could be a problem… My Mama says that men are all hard cocks and full balls. Hope you're wearing something loose.* She carried her mug back to her kitchen, ignoring his startled, outraged flash of temper. She spared a moment to consider notifying her parents or sibs that Dancer had arrived, but then she decided that she wanted to clarify things with him before adding the confusion of her family to the mix. Her brothers, in particular, could be quite protective. No, she would talk to him first. Let them settle their future without the well-meant interference from her family.

# Chapter Five

## ஐ

Eppie was backlit in the morning light in the circle entrance when Dancer caught his first glimpse of her. Immediately, he thought, *My God, she must be over six feet tall!*

When she stepped out onto the small lawn he forgot to breathe. She was *blue*. Her skin was a real pale shade of *blue*. He was positive it wasn't tattooed or some other form of body adornment because she was also completely *naked*. He could see her bare, puffy pussy lips. A *blue* pussy and lush generous curvy breasts with slightly darker blue nipples.

His mouth hung open. His startled green eyes met hers and he saw they were a deep, clear shade of turquoise that danced with amusement at his reaction. Without comment, she dropped the sandals she carried in one hand onto the grass at her feet, shook out the pale rose *meerlim* she carried over one arm and casually slipped it on. Self-consciously, she smoothed the tendrils at her neck and patted the intricate knotted arrangement of her lustrous black hair. Three slender jeweled picks anchored it at the crown of her head.

Then, she began to move toward him and his mouth snapped shut. She stalked with all the grace and queenliness of a hunting cat. This was not a woman to trifle with. Very carefully he noted the other details… Gently pointed ears with tiny gold hoops in the points, the intriguing tilt of her almond-shaped eyes and the hint of fanged eyeteeth. So—a predator lurked in her genes. He couldn't believe he'd made friends with a blue Vulcan.

While she joined him in the grassy circle, Eppie was making her own assessments. Her body sang with joy when she saw he was so tall and muscular. His long golden brown hair was neatly and properly confined in one braid that brushed below his butt. Glittering green eyes flashed with sharp intelligence and humor. And his face was both beautiful and masculine with a sturdy jaw and stubborn chin. Tiny green jewels adorned each earlobe.

"All men are *not* just hard cocks and full balls," he objected at once, reverting to their conversation.

She dropped her gaze to the front of his soft sweat pants and raised one eyebrow in query. The heavy bulge that tented them was obviously growing. "I would have no way of knowing about the full balls, but clearly the hard cock part is true—unless you out-valley men carry another type of weapon between your legs?"

Her bald comment left him stunned speechless. He pinched his nose and wondered if he would be able to ward off the migraine that was creeping up the back of his head. In all of their conversations, she had been completely, totally ladylike. This version of Eppie was not someone he was familiar with at all.

"Why are you acting like this? You never talked like this before! You were such a nice ladylike girl…"

"But obviously a nice ladylike girl didn't interest you," she pointed out. "You didn't want to bond with a *lady*."

"Can we start over?" he demanded in growing frustration.

"Certainly, if you wish. Where would you like to begin?"

Her calm, unconcerned demeanor just pissed him off. He snorted in disgust and waved one arm at the bench. "Have a seat. Obviously, I have some questions. Possibly, you have some answers. Perhaps you'll even be willing to share them with me."

"Of course. What would you like to know?" she inquired with irritating composure.

He sat down at the other end of the bench and stared at her, trying to decide where to begin. He had so many questions that hammered at him. Where was he? How had this happened to him? *Why* him and not some other guy? He began with the most puzzling bit of information she had shared. "Exactly what did you mean when you said that you would die if we didn't bond?"

She looked away for a moment, gathering her thoughts and then choosing her words with care she explained, "I have no knowledge of the out-valley, other than the things you have told me and the memories my parents have shared with us. In particular, they have discussed mating customs extensively. According to them, men are much like our valley men, but women are very different. If attraction exists, then a woman's body prepares her for sex and this may happen with any man. Is this correct?"

"Pretty much. Some women and men are more discriminating than others, but overall, that is true," he admitted.

"Odd. Here, it is not so. A woman must have an *attachment* or a formal bonding before her body will function in that way. And then she has no control over the way her body prepares her for sex. We call the process *schalzina*."

"*Schalzina*." He rolled the strange word over his tongue. "So get to the dying part."

"Once *schalzina* is fully fledged, the only relief is penetration and locking with her bond mate. If he isn't available in time, convulsions begin, leading to death." She shrugged and sighed. "Listening to myself explain this to you makes me see how strange you must find it."

"I'm pretty sure I understand the penetration part, but exactly what is locking?" he asked with dry trepidation.

"Near the womb, we have a ring of muscle called the *schela*. Once the depth of penetration is satisfactory, the *schela* tightens around the cock just behind the head, locking the male into position." She shot him a glance to check on his reaction to that bit of information and caught a most peculiar expression crossing his face—an odd mixture of fascination and horror.

"Uh-*huh*. And how long does this stage of the proceedings last?" he demanded with growing incredulity.

"It could be a short period, similar to normal sex between two partners. Or it could take a much longer time, like an afternoon or evening. Every woman is different. Every time is different," she clarified.

"Wait a minute. You have regular sex in addition to this *schalzina*?"

"*Schalzina* is related to the bonding process to aid conception. It's almost exclusively part of the process of conception. After the first child, it will not happen again until the woman's body is ready for pregnancy again."

Abruptly, he got to his feet and paced around the small lawn with his head bowed and his hands stuffed in his pockets. "Let me get this straight. Not only do you believe we are bond mates and need to bond immediately, but if all goes well, nine months from now we'll have a baby?"

"Actually," she corrected softly, "pregnancy in the valley is usually around seven moons."

"And a moon is what I would call a month?"

"Papa has said this is so," she agreed.

He stopped in front of her and tilted her head back with one finger so he could look her in the eyes. "What if I don't want to bond or have a child? What if I just want to go back where I came from? To tell you the truth, I wasn't looking for a woman. I just want someplace quiet to garden a little, try out new recipes and make some music."

"You will do what you will, of course," she replied after a brief hesitation. "And I will deal with what I must. I have no objection to music or cooking and I'm a gardener myself."

He didn't like her quiet acceptance. It wasn't normal. Plunging in, he determined to get more answers before they were interrupted. "How do you know we have an attachment?"

"We can mind talk. That only happens between two unrelated people who are either bonded or have an attachment." She hesitated before adding, "Also, I've already begun *schalzina*. It only happened when we talked. It's grown stronger each time you were on the mountain."

"That long? More than once?" he asked with mounting alarm as the true extent of her explanation dawned on him.

"Nearly three years… It's strong enough to be very uncomfortable." Shifting under his clear gaze, she twisted her hands together in her lap. Awkward did not begin to describe how she felt, trying to explain *schalzina*. It sounded so clinical when put into words. No wonder he wasn't very excited about bonding.

Sitting down next to her, he reached for her hands and held them between his. "How long until your time has run out, Eppie?" She tried to pull her hands away, but he just gently tightened his grip so she left them there, though she refused to meet his eyes. He shook her hands and ordered, "Answer me, Eppie. I think you owe me that much, at least."

With a shuddering sigh, she lifted her eyes to his, afraid of his reaction. "Perhaps an eight-day. Possibly less. Unless I go into *schalzah*."

"*Schalzah*. Exactly what is that? And how is it different from *schalzina*?"

"*Schalzah* is a sexual frenzy. You don't die from it, but Papa says that you might wish for death," she added with a small smile. "Usually both partners are drawn into *schalzah* and it lasts until the point of exhaustion. There is no true sense of completion."

Without releasing her hands, he sat back and pondered. One week to make a life decision. He could feel the stark tension in her hands and considered how very difficult this must be for her. Their proposed joining was less than romantic and because of his own lack of understanding he had inadvertently made her feel undesirable. "We still don't know each other very well," he said slowly. "I don't know much about this valley or what life will be like here. I would like to spend a couple days getting to know you better before I make any final decisions about this bonding you're talking about. Do you suppose we'll have that much time?"

She stared at him in open disbelief. "*Now* you're willing to be my bond mate? Why have you changed your mind?"

"Hmmm. Well, you're very beautiful, even if you do have blue skin and pointed ears," he teased gently. "And I've had quite a few less attractive offers. I can't say that I've had a burning desire for a child, but I don't have any major objections to the idea. And you've assured me that I have no way to return out-valley." He suddenly leaned forward and kissed her, savoring the softness of her lips, flicking her fangs with his tongue and feeling her shudder with arousal. "I've known several couples who had less to begin with. Do you think we can make it work?"

"If we swear the vows on the altar stone, we will have to make it work," she reminded him grimly. "It's a permanent bond that can only be broken by death."

"Well, then. Suppose you show me your valley and take me to meet your family?" He stood and pulled her to her feet.

With a very odd smile, she led the way around the outside of the circle. "This should be very interesting. I can't wait for you to meet Llyon and Tyger."

"*I* can't wait to meet your mother. She must be quite a woman."

\* \* \* \* \*

Out-valley, Traveller was facing his own difficulties. The hunt for the two brothers had intensified to the extent that Free

Llewellyn risked publicly accusing them of treason and murder. Trav sat in the living room of the tiny apartment that Dance had the foresight to rent years before under yet another identity. Dance's guitar and violin cases rested on the battered trunk in front of the couch that did double duty as a coffee table. The secret compartment in the guitar case was open and Trav was examining the papers he'd retrieved from it, hoping that Dance had left him some useful clues. When he opened the letter, he sighed with relief and hope.

*Trav —*

*If you're reading this, then I'll have to assume that my plans were at least partially successful. Enclosed are a map, keys for some spare vehicles, the key to another place in case you need it and personal papers — will, portfolio, banking stuff, etc.*

*Knowing exactly what an ass Free is, I'm going to guess that he will eventually make you part of his vendetta. On the enclosed CD you'll also find the evidence I've accumulated so far that points to him as the man behind our family's murders. It wouldn't stand up in court, but then I don't plan to take him to court!*

*Don't go off half-cocked and try to get him. I want to know WHY they were murdered and he can't tell us if he's dead. If you decide to follow me, be very careful. I don't plan to ever return to work for him. Know now that I'll die first. In case I don't see you again, I release you from your vow not to cut your hair. You may need to cut it short to change your appearance.*

*A floor safe is located under the dresser in the back room. It has a few things you might need if Free's declared open season. Feel free to use any of it — no pun intended.*

*I love you. Until we meet again —*

*Dance*

So. There it was in black and white. He examined the map carefully. There wasn't a single landmark on it that a stranger would recognize. Written and drawn in their private language, it revealed Dancer's target destination only for Trav. It was just one of several they had set up in the last few years.

He set the papers aside and immediately went to locate the safe. Its contents convinced him as nothing else would have that Dance had spent considerable time and thought planning his escape. He whistled softly through his teeth as he counted the money, stacked tidily in mixed bricks of $1000. Thirty-five bricks. No bills bigger than a twenty. No new bills. That required a *lot* of planning.

Arranged neatly next to the money was a variety of weapons, with ample appropriate ammunition, blank passports waiting for pictures and a lone key to an anonymous storage unit. As he sat on his heels, contemplating the contents of the safe, the itchy feeling that warned him of danger dramatically increased. Without further thought, he retrieved a heavy battered brown leather pack from the closet and emptied the safe before closing it and pushing the dresser back into place.

Moving swiftly, he gathered Dance's papers except for the map, shoved them back into the hidden compartment in the guitar case and locked the compartment. Then, pocketing the map and keys, he silently raised the bedroom window, stepped on the fire escape with his pack and the instrument cases and moved swiftly up to the roof.

From there, he patiently checked his back trail and observed the neighborhood. Within moments he had pinpointed the strangers. Flowing quietly across the roofs, he moved down the block until he reached a building containing a dry cleaners. He flipped up the trapdoor to the attic and dropped lightly inside with his baggage. Very softly, he closed and latched the door, before settling down to wait for his host. In a country very far away on a nasty, rainy night in a muddy alley, he had saved Chuin's life. He was safer in Chuin's attic than anywhere in the world.

Three days later the searchers finally moved on. Chuin drolly reported that they had carried off even the faded prints decorating the living room wall and the threadbare kitchen curtains. Hanky, one of the brightest kids on the block had spent hours loitering on his front steps, muttering an inventory into a pocket recorder as they emptied the apartment. When Trav listened to the running rap-like monologue later, he reflected that he hadn't paid Hanky nearly enough for his trouble.

They waited another four days before Chuin stashed Trav and his belongings in his closed panel van and drove to his cousin's warehouse. There Trav transferred to a battered gray Explorer, one of the vehicles Dancer had acquired. Soberly, he thanked Chuin for his assistance.

"We don't see each other again, I think," Chuin observed quietly. "Go with luck, Traveller."

"Take care, Chuin. Thank you for your help. Be careful. They may be back," Trav warned. "If they backtrack me to you, sing like a nightingale. Tell them everything you know. It won't hurt and it might even send them off down the wrong trail."

Chuin's black eyes glittered with unshed tears. "I will do what I must. Now, go!"

# Chapter Six

𝕾

As Eppie led him toward the village, Dancer noted signs of deer, rabbits, squirrels and birds populating the meadow they crossed. He noticed the butterflies floating from blossom to blossom. There appeared to be an abundance of game. No shortage of food here. He saw cherry, peach and apple trees. Pockets of blueberries vied with wild strawberries for room. Some butterflies seemed to follow them as they waded through the deep grasses. They came to a clear stream, stopping to taste the water. It was cold and sweet.

He squatted down and filled his water bottle with fresh water. Further down, he could see the stream was deeper, tumbling noisily over water-polished boulders. A frog, sunning on a rock near the bank, disappeared with a tiny splash. Crickets hummed drowsily in the warm grass. More butterflies — green, orange, yellow, blue, white, purple — flittered along in the high grass next to the stream.

They drifted into a stand of pine trees, absently avoiding a silver spider web, still glittering with drops of morning dew. The cool shade was surprisingly welcome after the unexpected heat of the open valley. Without a word of warning, he plopped down on a fallen log and faced the thoughts that had plagued him as they walked to Lost Market. Something was very odd in this valley. Here, it appeared to be high summer. On the outside, it was early winter. Either he had lost six months or he'd tumbled down Alice's rabbit hole. Nothing made sense.

Eppie sat down beside him and hesitantly asked, "Dancer? What's wrong?"

Perched on the log, he struggled to make sense of the things he observed. Plants were covered with ripe fruit out of season. While he was willing to admit that he didn't know every species, he had glimpsed some very strange flora and fauna on his short walk. "What is this place? Everything is so alien..."

"Papa and Mama said things have evolved differently here," she answered soberly. "When they first came, Papa thought they were on another planet. Ham and Nathan, a couple of scientists from out-valley that came before Mama and Papa, have a theory that there's a kind of portal in the tunnels, but then how could we have communicated over a long distance like that?"

He shook his head in confusion. "I don't know, Eppie. It was winter with blizzard conditions out-valley and here it's high summer. I just don't know what to think." Sighing deeply, he stood and pulled her to her feet. "Let's go and find your parents. Maybe they have some of my answers."

Thirty feet into the trees, they crossed the first active sign of human activity that Dancer had seen in the valley. It was a tiny clearing barely big enough to contain the stone cottage that sat squarely in the center of a small stone-walled yard. Window boxes on the two facing windows spilled bright pink and purple flowers over their edges. A heavy wooden Dutch door opened onto a small porch just wide enough to support a double hanging swing. As they approached, two young men came out onto the porch carrying what appeared to be bundles of bedding and dumped them in a small wood handcart.

He wanted to drift back into the trees and study them carefully, but Eppie tugged him forward with a quick smile. Within seconds he had deduced that they were identical twins, somewhere in their late teens or early twenties. It was difficult to judge with complete accuracy, but he suspected they were at least six inches over six feet tall. Both were shirtless, revealing broad muscular chests with long lean muscles in their arms. Their hair, an amazing shade of carrot red, was arranged in a multitude of narrow braids that fell well below their hips. Each braid ended in a square jeweled bead.

The bright red hair distracted him only for a moment from the smooth pale blue skin, pointed ears and dark tilted eyes. Broad intricate tattoo bands decorated their upper arms.

He was considerably taken aback by their clothing. Both wore wrapped skirts. There was no other way to say it. The skirts were too long and too full to be called kilts and ended just below their knees. The supple fabric fluidly flared around them as they worked. One wore blue, the other wore green. *Skirts.* Everything in him rebelled at the idea. Soft over-the-ankle boots that boasted embroidered cuffs of blue—and green—to match their skirts, completed the costumes.

He shook his head in dismay and felt an unaccountable urge to return immediately to the small cave behind the waterfall, but Eppie had his hand firmly clutched in hers and she tugged him into the clearing. "It's my brothers! Llyon! Tyger! Come meet Dancer!" she called out eagerly.

Tyger studied his potential bond brother with care. With approval, he saw that Dancer was his match in height and weight and carried himself confidently. Despite the stress of adjusting to his abrupt arrival in the valley, he was alert, ready to defend himself against the unknown. He offered a smile and said, "Welcome to the valley. When did you arrive?"

"Your time or mine?" Dancer countered with a cryptic smile.

Llyon grinned widely at his quick retort. "So—you're no pushover. Our time is the only thing that counts now."

"Early this morning, as far as I can tell. Eppie would be a better source of information."

"And you're not a chauvinist. That's a good sign," Tyger conceded. "What do you think of our valley?"

"I haven't seen much of it, so far, but what I've seen of it is very beautiful. It's a lovely place to visit—I just didn't plan to be a permanent resident." He looked around the clearing with deepening curiosity. "What is this place?"

Llyon choked briefly, shot a querying glance at Eppie and then answered with disarming frankness, "This is a bonding cottage. If you decide to bond with Eppie, this will be your residence for the next three or four moons."

It was Dancer's turn to catch his breath at Llyon's bluntness before admitting, "We're discussing it. There are still some things I need to know."

Llyon nodded agreeably. "Just don't take too long," he warned. "Eppie's time is running out. I wouldn't want to have to kill you for letting my sister die."

A brief shocking silence ensued as his words hung in the air. Then for the first time in their encounter, Dancer offered a genuine smile. "You remind me of my brother, Trav. I think you two would get on like a house afire. Too bad you won't be able to meet him."

"I would never say that won't happen," Tyger drawled lazily. "Stranger things have occurred."

"I can't think of much that would be stranger than my day so far. Come on Eppie. We need to get on our way." Dancer latched a gentle hand around her upper arm and gave a little tug. "How far away is this village of yours?"

The twins couldn't hear her muttered reply, but it didn't matter. They were more interested in the body language between the stranger and their sister. And that told them that they needed to get busy and finish their work.

Ly and Ty went back into the cottage to complete their cleaning tasks. If all went well Dancer and their sister would be living here in the bonding cottage called Stonehollow very soon. "So what do you think?" asked Ty as he cleaned the small bathing room with meticulous care.

"He's appalled by our *shardas*," Llyon replied succinctly.

Ty laughed very quietly. "Shall we wager on how long it takes him to give up his pants?"

Llyon paused in his sweeping and gave the idea some consideration. "What will we wager?"

"Hah! If I win, no dishes for a week."

"All right," Ly agreed readily. "If I win, you cook for a week."

"Llyon!"

"Tyger! Don't wager if you aren't ready to pay!"

"Oh, very well. Agreed," Ty replied sulkily. "I think he'll not wear the *sharda* until they've completed their seclusion."

"No? How will he take care of her during *schalzina*?" Ly wondered aloud.

"They'll be alone at the cottage," Tyger pointed out. "Why would they need any clothes?"

"Well," Ly acknowledged reluctantly, "that is true. The weather will be warm now that summer is here." He finished his sweeping and went to make the bed.

"So when do you say?" Ty asked slyly, while he folded and hung the bathing sheets.

"Hmm. Well, I think he'll wear it on the day of their oath binding. I think he'll do it to please her." He tucked in the coverlet and fluffed the pillows. "I hope he will want to please her. She's waited a very long time for him."

Tyger leaned against the doorjamb, silently watching him finish up. Gathering up their cleaning supplies, he led the way outside. "If he wears it on their oath-binding day to please her, I'll cook without complaining. She has waited a long time," he agreed soberly. "A very long time."

The path that led to the village wandered through a new section of woods. Immediately, Dancer knew that he was in a fantasy forest. As they walked along the trail, he took note of the plants, both familiar and strange. Unlike the last stand of trees he'd encountered, most of these were very strange, indeed. There were huge trees with odd dark blue leaves. One lonely tree had smooth, glittery black bark. Back from the path, he saw a pair of trees with orange bark and triangular purple leaves. Occasionally, he spotted pine-like trees with shiny red needles. The undergrowth was a multi-colored riot of prolifically flowering shrubs and a bright blue runner vine. Suddenly, without warning, the path took a sharp jog to the right and they stood at the edge of a thriving village unlike anything he had ever seen.

Circular adobe homes with smooth, domed adobe roofs were arranged in concentric circles around a cluster of larger circular domed buildings. The domes ranged from small, one circle homes to a very large compound of multiple joined domes.

Without hesitation, Eppie headed for the compound. Following on her heels, he observed as much as he could, noting the neat yards and gardens enclosed with low stone walls. Some had blue or green birds similar to chickens pecking at the dirt. In a couple of yards, enormous long-haired creatures that vaguely resembled dogs, silently eyed them as they walked by.

On the front steps of the compound, two huge cat-like animals were curled up, sleeping in the sun. The long-haired orange one's ears twitched as they went by and it opened one green eye before settling back into slumber. The chocolate and cream animal opened both eyes, yawned mightily, revealing a mouth full of sharp teeth and stretched before curling back up and snoring lightly. "Those are Tyger and Llyon's *packits*," Eppie commented briefly before opening the door and entering the cool darkness of a wide foyer.

Dancer merely nodded and followed her inside, completely resigned to the odd and amazing. It took his eyes a moment to adjust to the shadowy hallway, but when they did, he observed a entryway like he had never imagined. A huge exquisite woven tapestry covered the wall on the left. The deep jewel colors shone vividly, even in the dimness. On the right, three unframed landscapes were arranged above a long narrow carved table. There were no artist names on the paintings, but it was obvious the same individual—in a style reminiscent of Goya—had painted them all. Bold bright colors portrayed life in the valley. The table below them had elaborately carved legs and skirt. When he bent over to study it, he saw the carvings were leaves and flowers.

Eppie barely paused before leading him into a larger room with an empty fireplace and a large varied collection of chairs. Standing in the doorway, he stared around in amazement. Every chair was occupied. Near the center of the room, he picked out two people he thought must be her parents. After focusing for a moment, he realized the rest were probably her siblings...and there were a lot of them. Every single male, from the youngest through the eldest, was dressed in the skirt-like garments. Some had on loose over-wrapped shirts, but most were bare-chested. And all of them had their hair neatly arranged in the narrow braids ending with the tiny jeweled clasps.

The man in the center stood and came forward, offering his hand in a gesture that was the first familiar thing Dancer had encountered. They shook hands as the man said, "Welcome. I'm Merlyn, that's my wife Jade," he nodded toward a very youthful looking redhead, "and the rest are our children, who I won't overwhelm you further by introducing."

"I appreciate that," Dancer replied dryly.

"Come in and rest," Jade invited with a lovely smile. "Arturo, please bring tea and wafers. The rest of you may satisfy your curiosity later. I'm sure you all have someplace to be. If not, I'll be happy to find something for you to do." In seconds, the room echoed with emptiness as they quietly vanished.

Unable to help himself, Dancer began to laugh. "I've never seen a room empty so fast."

"Well-ll. I'm sure things are overwhelming enough without being stared at," Jade pointed out with a grin. "It's been a while since Merlyn and I arrived, but I remember very well the difficulties of adjusting to the strangeness."

He and Eppie followed Merlyn to the chairs grouped around Jade and made themselves comfortable. Twin young men appeared with trays of red pottery mugs of steaming tea, a pale green pot of honey and thin wafers arranged on a deep blue pottery plate. As they served, Eppie introduced them. "These are my brothers, Arturo, on your right and Arano, to your left. And this is my friend, Dancer."

Arturo nodded wordlessly and retreated back to the kitchen, but Arano offered his hand for a friendly shake. "Welcome. If I can help you in any way, please let me know," he offered before following his brother.

They sipped their tea in a comfortable silence and allowed Dancer to slowly relax before Merlyn inquired quietly, "Have you and Eppie talked about the bonding?"

Dancer nodded. "We discussed it before we came here. I still have some questions and reservations, but I'm not willing to let her die because of that."

Jade cocked her head to one side as though listening to another conversation. After a moment, she asked, "Can we help you with anything? Adjusting to the customs and mores of the valley can be complicated without guidance."

Involuntarily, he blurted out, "What's with the braids and skirts?" Then in acute embarrassment, he snapped his mouth shut as his face turned a ruddy red.

Eppie and her parents all grinned and Eppie admitted, "I've been told that the men all want to know about that first. I confess that I don't see the problem, but Papa will be able to help you with that. Mama, why don't we go out into the garden so they have privacy for the questions Dancer needs to ask?"

It was only as Eppie unobtrusively led Jade from the room that Dancer realized that she must be blind. "She's blind." The flat tone of his voice revealed his shock.

"Yes. It happened in an accident the last time we looked for an exit from the valley just before Arano and Arturo were born. She nearly lost the twins in a fall. After that, we decided that we would be content with our lot here. No chance of returning to the out-valley was worth the loss of her sight."

What was there to say to that? Dancer nodded solemn agreement and waited for Merlyn to speak.

# Chapter Seven

ॐ

Sitting back in his chair, Merlyn marshaled his thoughts before attempting to answer Dancer's burning questions. He knew that his future bond son felt silly for asking them, but in truth, the answers were important. "You asked about our clothing and hair arrangements…"

Waving it away, Dancer said, "Never mind. It was stupid."

"No. No, it's actually quite important that you understand. I find myself trying to decide how to best convey the importance of our dress and customs." He leaned forward, clasping his large hands between his knees and studied Dancer intently. "This will require a suspension of your current reality," he warned. "The valley has no formal government, police system or army. It's a small place, actually. Dai, my mentor and the senior healer in the valley and I have walked the entire valley. As closely as I can ascertain, it's roughly seventy miles across—in any direction. Our last census two years ago revealed a population just over fifteen hundred people. As you saw in your walk here, much of the valley is meadows or woods and unpopulated."

"That's not many people for that much territory," Dancer observed slowly.

"No. If you consider that over half of them have more than sixty years, then you can see the consequences. There is a very small reproductive aged pool."

"Interbreeding?"

"None in the last six hundred years," Merlyn explained. "At that time, for reasons Dai and I cannot understand, tough restrictions were set in place to prevent that. But, in the last fifty years, that has become the least of the problems in the valley."

"And what is the problem now?" Dancer demanded uneasily.

"Now, with the exception of the newest arrivals in the valley, pregnancies are rare. The last babies born in the valley were my own children, Cougar and Gazelle, born seven years ago."

He sighed and added, "Hamilton McCrory and his wife, Rebaccah, have four children. Nathan and Morgana Taylor have three. With extremely rare exceptions, no other couples have more than two."

"And what about you and Jade?"

Merlyn's cheeks blushed a faint shade of violet and he coughed. "We have fourteen," he admitted with embarrassed pride.

"You don't expect Eppie and me to have fourteen?" Dancer demanded in alarm.

"Well-ll no. I would be happy with one. Of course, it's really not up to me—or you, for that matter. There are no actual birth control devices in the valley and no need for them."

"So, a man from out-valley is a blessing because he might father three, or even more children." Dancer considered the odd position of being cast as a potential father. It boggled the mind to be wanted not for his money or influence or talents, but because of his sperm count. "What does your population problems have to do with the skirts and hairdo?"

"Eppie explained *schalzina*?"

"Yeah. Now that's some weird shit, but not as weird as that *schalzah*. Does Jade have this *schalzina* too?"

Merlyn pursed his lips. "Fourteen children," he offered briefly as confirmation.

"Oh, yeah. I guess she does." Dancer stared at him morosely. "How do you know she wants you just for you?"

"Once you have your oath-binding, you'll be able to feel what she feels. You'll know the difference," Merlyn assured him. "There won't be any doubt at all."

"The skirts?"

"We call them *shardas*. If you know about *schalzina*, you know the importance of immediate *availability*," Merlyn said delicately. "The bonding cottages are one way to provide extensive privacy. But the time will come when you might be, say out on a walk, with Eppie when *schalzina* begins. Your *sharda* provides immediate availability without leaving your ass hanging out in the wind," Merlyn ended bluntly.

Presented with that vivid image, Dancer nodded understanding. "That's why her dress is designed like it is?"

"Exactly. They're called *meerlims*. With practice, you can deal with *schalzina* without any private portion of your bodies visible. I won't say that an observer couldn't tell what you were doing—but they won't *see* what you're doing—which is the point."

"How often does that happen?"

"Not as often as it used to," Merlyn admitted sadly. "*Schalzina* is necessary for pregnancy to occur and successfully continue. For some reason, that's not happening, though I'm positive it will with you and Eppie."

Dancer sighed rather gustily and absently picked up a couple of wafers from the tray. "Don't tell me the hairdos have some weird place in *schalzina*..."

Merlyn grinned suddenly. "No, they don't. Nothing kinky with the hair—unless you want it that way. I'm not going to get into that. The hair arrangements are significant in another way. I started to explain about the law enforcement in the valley."

Dancer cocked his head. "You said there wasn't any."

"Not exactly. There is a warrior caste here. They serve as police, justices and army. The braids and the *chinkas* at the ends denote rank, training and talents." Merlyn stood and gestured with his mug. "I'm going to get another mug of tea. Would you like more?"

"Sure." Dancer got to his feet and stretched. "If you don't mind, I'll come with you."

"Come along, then," Merlyn replied agreeably. "I'll introduce you to the most important room in the house."

"The bathroom?"

"On the way. To the kitchen."

\* \* \* \* \*

In the back garden, Jade sat in a deeply slanting chair that she and Merlyn called an Adirondack chair. It had taken them some time and effort to convince Eron, the woodworker, that it was exactly what they wanted. Once he tried it out himself, he had fashioned two more and set them outside his workshop. Soon their popularity spread across the valley so that now, nearly every garden boasted at least one or two.

Eppie happily weeded the garden while they discussed Dancer's arrival in the valley. "Are you content with your agreement?" Jade asked curiously.

"Yes. Strangely enough, I trust him more because he's expressed his doubts. If he had agreed at once to our bonding with no reservations, I think I would have been uneasy." She tossed another weed in her gathering basket and sat back on her heels. "Mama, he's a strong-willed man. If he decides to adjust to the ways of the valley, he will likely do it with his whole heart. I would rather have a steadfast man that was a friend, than a wishy-washy lover."

"How did he react to your explanation of *schalzina*?"

Eppie laughed very quietly. "With interest."

"Indeed. I don't think you're talking about intellectually. So, will he be capable of pleasing you?"

"Judging by the amount of interest he displayed, I would say that I will be more than pleased," Eppie concurred happily. "Very, very pleased."

"Well, then. What more could you want?" Imperceptibly, Jade relaxed. "Love will grow as you spend time together. Friendship is more important in the beginning. And *schalzina* will ensure passion at the start of your relationship. By the time your first child is born, you will have developed the feelings you need to continue."

"I don't think a lack of passion is going to be a problem," Eppie retorted dryly, remembering the taste of his kiss.

\* \* \* \* \*

Merlyn pointed out the bathing-room to Dancer and went to the kitchen to wait for him. When Dancer arrived, hovering in the doorway, Merlyn waved him in and set two steaming mugs on the table. "Come on in. Any time you're in our home, you will likely be in this room, so make yourself comfortable."

Staring around the large room, Dancer took in the huge wooden table and chairs—enough for a family of sixteen to sit more than comfortably—and shook his head in wonderment. On one wall a large, heavy cabinet held an assortment of pottery dishes, odd cutlery and curiously shaped glasses. Another wall was covered with shelves that held pottery and glass canisters. In the far corner, an odd sink and counter arrangement incorporating a strange stovetop ran from the back door to a open doorway that offered a glimpse of some type of treatment room. He noted the absence of any type of refrigerator. A couple of extra chairs sat on either side of the dish cabinet.

Merlyn studied the room, trying to see it through Dancer's eyes. "A little strange?"

"Some. No refrigerator?"

"No," Merlyn agreed. "No electricity, for one thing. There are very few perishables. They're kept in the springhouse and fetched as needed. Meats are kept in the smokehouse. Almost everything else is canned or dried."

Dancer moved into the room and picked a place at the table. "I noticed that you have running water…"

Laughing heartily, Merlyn nodded. "That was one of the first innovations that Nathan, Ham and I worked on. Our wives were *very* demonstrative about their gratitude. Since then, most of the valley has accepted that adaptation. We're careful about the innovations we introduce to the valley and how they will change the culture."

"I wondered about that," Dancer replied quietly. "Nathan and Hamilton's names sound vaguely familiar to me."

"Nathan and Hamilton were very important, famous scientists before they came here. Their disappearance provoked a furor. You would have been quite young then, but major events do impress themselves on even the young."

"That could be it. You and Jade also seem strangely familiar. At first I thought it was because Eppie looks so much like you, but now, I'm not so sure."

"Well, no doubt you will figure it all out, eventually," Merlyn observed mildly. "Now, perhaps you will tell me what catastrophe brought you to our valley."

"A tunnel."

"That I know about. What happened before that to send you on retreat?"

Dancer stared at his mug as though the secrets of the valley were all there for his taking. How much to tell Merlyn? How would he react to Dancer's past life? He cricked his neck, trying to relieve some of the sudden tension. Then, in a rush of sudden need to unburden himself, he decided to share it all with the man sitting patiently across from him.

"Before I came here," he began haltingly, "I was an assassin for the federal government under the direction of a man named Free Llewellyn. As a cover, I spent a great deal of time touring as a soloist musician, violin, guitar and occasionally, mandolin."

Merlyn's entire body went still when he heard his father's name. So the old man was still alive, still in power, and still ruining anyone who got in his way. He suppressed the shudder that memories of his father always triggered. "That must have been very difficult. You don't strike me as a man who kills easily."

"It was," Dancer admitted. "Finally, a time came when my mission was compromised and children were used as hostages to prevent me from taking out my target. I scrubbed the mission, but Free sent in a second team and they took them all out—including the children."

"I imagine that was very hard to take. But other men have had to deal with similar betrayal. There must have been something else that was the final straw."

"You're very insistent," Dancer suspiciously observed with an annoyed frown.

"May as well get it all out. Then you won't have anything to hide from Jade or me. We have a lot of experience with that sort of thing from dealing with our children."

"You are an odd piece of work."

Merlyn chuckled. "If you agree to bond with Eppie, then you'll be our son. And we'll treat you the same way."

"I'm too old to be your son," Dancer objected shortly. "I bet you aren't even fifty."

"Nah...Jade and I are older than dirt. At least there are days we feel that way." He snagged a squat pottery jug from the dish cabinet and set it on the table between them. "Have a cookie. It will make it easier to tell me."

"Is that part of your parental technique? Your kids must have *beaucoup* cavities."

"There are no cavities in the valley. And no gum disease. I think it's something in our DNA once we transform."

"No kidding? No cavities?"

"None."

Helping himself to a cookie, Dancer stared at Merlyn and debated about telling him the rest. Finally, with a small shake of his head, he revealed, "Just over a year ago, my parents and siblings were murdered while my oldest brother, Trav and I were on a mission. Trav knows about the cave I was going to, so he will show up there eventually. He was planning to resign also. Then we were going to decide on a place to retire to."

"Ahhh. So we may have Trav as a new arrival, also. That will be nice," Merlyn replied placidly. "I'll have to warn the others, in case he shows up."

"Fuck! Nothing bothers you?"

"The 'F' word is still around?" Merlyn countered with a reminiscent smile.

"Oh, yeah. Now it's a noun, verb, adverb, adjective and expletive. The all-purpose word. Some of the younger set use it for a complete sentence without using any other words," he informed Merlyn with a sour smile. "You hear it everywhere— shopping, traveling, in line at the McDonald's."

"That must be disconcerting. What do people with children do?"

"You don't understand…it's the *kids* using the word. Five- and six-year-olds," he clarified.

"Now that's disgusting." Merlyn stared at him with disapproval. "What are their parents thinking of?"

"Don't look at me! I don't curse in front of kids." He stood and restlessly paced around the room. "Can we go find Eppie now?"

"In a few minutes. Aside from bonding with my daughter, what are your plans for your future?"

"How the hell would I know?" Dancer demanded irritably. "I play music and kill people. It doesn't seem to me that there's much call for either skill here in your little lost utopia."

"I wouldn't say that. We have a great need for a capable trainer for our warriors. I suspect that your skills are more than equal to that task. And we've had a need for music for a long time. Over the past few years, I've taken to collecting any old instruments I could find. When things settle down after your oath-binding, maybe you'll want to look at them and see if any are suitable for the purpose of training our valley children."

"If I'm to support your daughter, what I need is a job, not just make-work to keep me busy." Dancer sat back and drummed his fingers restlessly on the table. "This just sucks. There's nothing here for me to do except this weird bonding with your daughter. You can only spend so much time fucking. Surely there are other, more suitable men in this valley?"

"None that she wanted," Merlyn pointed out dryly. "Since the women make that choice here, I believe that you're stuck. But we have a barter system here, Dance. Teachers are highly regarded and are afforded high credit for their skills. If you choose to teach either warrior skills to our older young men or music to our youngsters, you will make more than enough barter credit to cover your family's needs."

"Maybe. I'll think about it. Can we go find Eppie *now*?"

Merlyn shoved his chair back and placed the cookie jug back in the cabinet, hiding a small smile. He judged that Eppie would be bonded with Dancer in the next two or three days because clearly, *schalzina* wasn't the only thing that bound them together.

* * * * *

After a dinner filled with strange pungent tastes and the unfamiliar din of seventeen people all talking at once, Dancer was more than ready to retire to someplace quiet. Without explanation, Eppie silently led him outside and down the path to the edge of the village. Soft night sounds soothed him as she twisted on her lightstone and headed into the woods. Curiously uncurious and exhausted by his long eventful day, he ambled along, content with their comfortable silence. About ten minutes later, they entered a small clearing with a cabin situated in the center. In the faint moonlight, he made out a tiny garden to one side, fenced in with rough poles. The cabin had a small porch with a neat flower-lined walkway leading up to the steps.

When they went up the steps and into the cabin, he realized that the interior was one large room, divided by clever arrangement of the furniture into living, sleeping and eating areas. He surmised that the door next to the fireplace led to the bathroom. While he stood just inside the doorway, familiarizing himself with her cabin, Eppie moved around it, twisting lightstones on and shoving random furniture pieces out of the way. Then, she pulled a long drawer at the base of her high bed out and he saw that it was some type of trundle bed. Moving quickly to help her, they positioned it in the space she had created by moving the furniture. She directed him to the bathing room, explaining, "You might want a shower before you sleep. Ly and Ty brought your pack out here this afternoon. It should be tucked in the corner cabinet."

Without surprise, he located the cabinet, extracted his pack and made his way into the bathroom, closing the door behind him. While he cleaned up, Eppie made up the trundle bed and began preparations for breakfast. Mixing *peekie* eggs, goat milk and pieces of tough, chewy sunflower bread together, she set it aside while she minced a mild pepper and a small precious *draka*. After tossing them together with the egg mixture, she poured it into a greased pottery casserole and carried it out to her spring house to keep it cool overnight. In the morning, it would be ready to bake.

Just as she came back into the house, Dancer opened the bathing room door, allowing a billow of fragrant steam to escape. "Eppie? Do you have a razor I can use? I left mine back in the cave."

Cautiously, she poked her head through the door and inquired, "What is a razor?"

"Whiskers," he replied succinctly. "I need a razor to shave—remove the whiskers."

She admired the long muscled line of his back and the taut fit of the bathing sheet over his curved ass before noting the rampant dragon tattoo on his shoulder with widening eyes.

He cleared his throat and commented dryly, "The hair I need to remove is on my face."

Lifting her gaze to meet his, a small smile crept across her face. "I can see that." She reached around him and picked up a small blue pot from the shelves on the wall. "Use this."

When he just stood looking at it in puzzlement, she removed the lid and dipped her fingers into the soft blue salve it contained. Then she slathered it over his cheek and jaw. "Now, wash it off," she directed, distracted by the warm musky male smell.

He wiped the salve from his face and was amazed when smooth, hairless skin was all that was left. "What is this stuff?"

"Hair remover?"

"Very funny. Okay, get out while I finish up in here."

She closed the wooden lid on the toilet seat and sat down. "Why? Do you have something I can't see? You saw all of me this morning..."

"And that was certainly quite a shock! What did you think you were doing?" he demanded as he finished wiping the salve from his face. He fingered his jaw and shook his head in wonderment. "How long does it take for the hair to grow back?"

"About an eight-day."

"Why were you naked this morning?"

"Because I came through the bonding circle," she explained calmly. "Normally, no clothing is allowed in the circle except in an emergency," she amended. "This morning was not an emergency."

Dancer stood there staring down at her with the washcloth clutched in his strong fingers. "Didn't you tell me that we bond in the circle?"

"That why it's called a bonding circle."

"Naked? We bond naked?"

# Chapter Eight

Eppie gave the bathing sheet a little twitch and it slid to the floor, leaving him completely bare for her delighted inspection. Virginal didn't mean that she was completely innocent. In the valley, extensive sex education taught by the healers was mandatory. Every effort was made for bondings to be contented and happy pairings. Eppie took his rapidly hardening cock in tender hands and with a gentle tug, pulled him in front of her. He groaned and placed his hands on her shoulders, holding her away. "Eppie, if you plan to wait until our bonding, then you can't be playing with my cock."

Slipping through his fingers, she leaned forward, taking a leisurely swipe over the broad head with her questing tongue. Tilting her head back to look him in the eye, she said, "Final consummation will have to wait, but there's no reason why we can't get to know each other a little. I've waited for you a long time and I'm hungry. You taste wonderful." She leaned forward and slid him between her lips, savoring the taste and scent of him with her tongue. Deeply conscious of her own body's preparations, she knew she was swollen and wet, but the hard, demanding contractions of *schalzina* were completely absent. This was desire, pure and simple.

Dancer spread his legs and braced himself with a hand on the doorjamb, unable to tear himself away. He would have never dreamed that he would be standing here enjoying Eppie suck his cock so deliciously—never in a million years. Reluctantly, through gritted teeth, he panted, "What about *schalzina*? Will this set it off?"

Without releasing his hot, throbbing flesh, she slowly shook her head. He thrust deeper into her mouth and she swallowed him with ease, squeezing him in her throat before allowing him to withdraw slightly. Soft fingers stole down below his cock and played with his balls. His thrusts came quicker as he helplessly gave in to her ministrations. Then she hummed around his cock as she swallowed it and the vibrations sent shock waves to the base of his spine. Gasping, he warned, "I'm going to come now, Eppie."

Grasping his firm ass in her warm hands, she held him in place as he groaned and shot pulse after pulse of hot semen down her throat. When he emptied his balls, he slumped back against the jamb. She gave him one last loving suckle and then licked him clean. Dancer was shocked when he felt himself getting hard again from her tender attentions. Pulling away, he sighed deeply and said, "Enough. Just wait a minute."

With a pout that bordered on sulkiness, Eppie sat back and growled, "What? Didn't you like it?" She eyed his cock, still dark rose and shiny from her wet tongue. The head bobbed as it continued to lengthen.

He choked out a laugh. "I certainly liked it, as you are very well aware. But it's my turn to play now." Pulling her to her feet, he tugged at the fastenings of her *meerlim* and slid it from her shoulders when they came loose. It fell in a puddle of soft fabric at her feet, leaving her as naked as she had been when he first saw her. "No underwear, I see," he noted with a satisfied smile.

"Underwear?" Her breathing seemed to stop when he gently pinched her nipples and tugged them to hard, sensitive points.

"Uh-hmm. Something you wear under your outer wear." He leaned forward and took one nipple in his hot wet mouth and suckled hard. Her knees wobbled and she would have slipped back down to sit on the toilet, but he held her up with surprising strength by wrapping one arm around her waist.

Hazily, she thought she was supposed to be answering a question, but for the life of her, she couldn't remember what it was. He switched breasts and she moaned, pressing closer as she felt the urgent nudge of his cock between her legs, rubbing the slippery swollen lips.

Raising his head, he looked at her face with deep satisfaction and announced, "Time to find a bed." She made no objection as he led her to her bed and helped her up onto the high surface before joining her. With a gentle shove, he arranged her like he wanted and sprawled between her spread legs. Abruptly, he was struck by a desire he had never felt before. Perhaps it was because he had no control over his life in the present, but he felt the need to restrain her — the need for her to trust him to be in complete control. Rearing up, he demanded, "How much do you trust me, Eppie?"

"What?" Her confusion was plain on her face.

"I want to restrain you and pleasure you," he explained cautiously. "Do you trust me enough to do that?"

"Restrain me?"

"Tie you up," he elaborated. "Just your hands. If you're afraid, that's okay. We won't do it."

The idea of being under his total control was unexpectedly exciting. She could feel herself getting wetter as a picture of herself restrained filled her mind. Unable to speak, she nodded her head and watched him curiously as he went to his pack and rummaged for a few minutes before returning to the bed with a heavy white sock and a long skinny piece of flexible material. Kneeling with one knee on each side of her torso, he held both hands in one of his, clasping them together and briefly ordered, "Keep them like that." Then he tied them together with the soft sock, not too tightly, but firmly enough that she couldn't pull them apart. Looping the long skinny object through the sock, he wound it around one of her wooden bed rails and slipped the end through a tiny slot she hadn't noticed and pulled it snug. The taut pull of her arms held over her head lifted her breasts. Her nipples tightened sharply in anticipation.

"What is that?"

"It's a tie-wrap. The police use them as temporary handcuffs for prisoners sometimes." In his position, his cock was close enough for her to reach with her mouth and she stuck out her tongue for a long slow lick. He inhaled sharply and pulled away. "Enough of that, baby. It's my turn to lick you. Let's see if I can give you as much pleasure as you gave me." Moving back down her body, he settled between her legs and gently spread her swollen petals apart. "Ahhh. A pretty blue flower, opening just for me." With one long swipe, his tongue washed her from her anus to her clit. She arched up in shock. Lifting his head to check her expression, he nodded once and returned for another determined pass. If he had his way, she would be one happy, satisfied woman when they finally slept.

Hours later, Eppie woke with a deep shudder as a warm wet tongue pierced her entrance, gently fucking her sensitive flesh. Over the hours, Dancer had rearranged her several times, always reapplying the restraints before pleasuring her in each new position until she slid into an exhausted sleep. Each time, she woke in a new position with his mouth and hands busily arousing her to new heights of passion. He had even placed her on her belly and fucked her pussy and ass together with his fingers. She felt a vague sense of naughtiness because of the extreme pleasure it gave her.

"Dancer?" She was shocked at the gravelly sound of her own voice. Probably all that screaming she'd done.

"Hmmm?"

"When will it be my turn again?"

"Tomorrow?" he replied absently as he very gently licked the creases in the folds between her legs and then suckled each of the swollen lips of her labia.

"Isn't it tomorrow yet?" she asked on a soft gasp.

"Nope. Not yet. Just relax and enjoy. I'll tell you when it's your turn."

"Do I get to tie you up?" she demanded with a sudden gleam in her eye.

"If you want to," he agreed after a long moment. "I've never been tied up like that. I trust you not to hurt me."

"Not much, anyway," she teased before giving herself up to his ministrations.

The next time she woke, they were spooned together in the disheveled bed with Dancer's hard cock lodged between her legs, against the slick folds of her pussy. He snored lightly below her ear and she smiled at this endearing, unexpected imperfection. The sun was high enough in the sky to indicate midmorning.

Moving carefully, she slipped from his embrace and slid from the bed. Padding into the bathing room, she looked at herself in the mirror. She certainly looked well-loved. Sometime in the night, Dancer had pulled the carved skewers from her hair. Black silky curls tumbled down her back nearly to her knees in tangled profusion. Her nose twitched and wrinkled. She smelled well-loved, too. Time for a shower and then she would start breakfast. Her busy, inventive man should be hungry when he woke up. She blushed when she remembered some of the things he had done to her. Definitely time for a shower.

When she was dressed, she went out to the spring house to retrieve the casserole she had prepared the night before. Somehow, it came as no surprise when she found Llyon waiting patiently for her on the back steps when she returned. He inspected her carefully before nodding. "You look very pleased with yourself," he observed.

"I am," she admitted. "What brings you out here this morning?"

"It's nearly noon."

"And you felt compelled to point this out because?"

"Eppie," he replied patiently, "I'm your healer. I'm concerned about you. Are you all right?"

"I'm still a virgin. I've broken no laws," she said stiffly.

"But you're not entirely untouched either. I wasn't asking you if you were. It's none of my business. I'm more interested in *schalzina*."

She sat down on the steps next to him with the casserole cradled in her lap. "Llyon, it seems to have faded." Her brows puckered in puzzlement. "Right before he came to the valley, the contractions were getting so strong they were quite painful. Now, since he's finally here, they've faded away. I don't understand why."

"I spoke to Dai this morning. He said this might happen. Especially, if you and Dancer find other ways to relieve some of the um, tension." He stretched out an arm and hugged her. "It appears that you can delay things a bit by indulging in a little play. So, I wish you joy, sister."

He stood and straightened his *sharda* before loping down the stairs and across the clearing.

She rose and went back into the cabin to find an empty bed and the sound of the shower running. She sprinkled cubes of soft orange *rowan* cheese over the top of the casserole and checked the temperature of the hearth oven. It was hot enough. After slipping the casserole in her oven, she went to the bed and stripped the sheets off, dumping them in her wash tub before hunting out a clean set and remaking the bed. She was tucking in the last corner of the quilt when he opened the door and strolled out into the main room stark naked with his damp golden hair streaming down his back.

She surveyed his body, starting at the top and slowly working her way down to his toes. Then her hot gaze returned to his groin where dark gold curls surrounded his half-erect cock. Her mouth watered in anticipation as she moved to meet him. He quirked an eyebrow in question as she gently pushed him down into a deep stuffed chair. Without a word, she parted his knees and knelt down, curling comfortably between his legs, before taking his cock in her soft hands and planting hot, wet sucking kisses from the base of the shaft to the wide, fat head. By the time she was finished, he was rigidly erect and flushed deep pink. Clear drops dribbled from the tip.

"My turn," she declared with satisfaction. And with one gulp, she seemed to swallow him whole.

He moaned. "Fuck, yeah." He shelved his plans for exploring the valley with her without a backward glance. Hell, the valley would be here tomorrow. Or the day after that. When she clamped the muscles in her throat around him like a vise, he widened his legs in involuntary invitation and decided the valley could wait until next year. No hurry. There was nothing he really wanted to see right now except Eppie kneeling in front of him with his cock buried in her mouth.

She tormented him mercilessly, backing off when he neared completion and then noisily sucking and licking him with enthusiasm. She tickled his balls and rolled them gently in her fingers. One stealthy finger penetrated his ass. Finally, groaning and panting, he begged, "Please, Eppie. Now, now, now! Now!" he shouted as he flooded her mouth with his hot come.

She meticulously licked him clean before resting her head on his thigh and sighing. He buried his hands in her hair, using it to pull her into his lap and crushed her mouth beneath his. He could taste himself on her tongue as they leisurely explored each other. Eventually, he pulled back and cradled her head against his shoulder with one hand while he plucked at the fastening of her *meerlim*.

"How are you feeling this morning?" he teased gently.

"Wonderful." He could feel her smile against his collarbone. "Llyon asked the same thing."

"Llyon!" He sat up in alarm, but she leaned against him, pushing him back.

"He's been and gone. Relax."

"What did he say?"

"That I looked happy. And that Dai told him that some gentle play between us might delay *schalzina* for a few days." She yawned and then sighed. "You exhausted me, you demon. I think we'll need a nap this afternoon during the nooning rest."

"Nooning rest?"

"After lunch, everyone spends the hottest part of the day inside resting."

"Out-valley they call that a siesta," he said. "It's a wonderful custom. Can we begin a little early?"

"Not until after we have something to eat. We both expended a lot of energy last night, even if it was wonderful. I just want to stay right here until breakfast is ready." She yawned again and wriggled until she was comfortably sprawled against his broad chest.

With a little grin, he rubbed his cheek against the top of her head. "So all it takes to get you in a good mood is great sex, huh?"

"That's right," she agreed slurring her words as she drifted into sleep.

He wondered how he was supposed to know that breakfast was done. He could smell something delicious cooking in the kitchen. Reluctantly, he shook her awake. "Eppie, how am I supposed to know when breakfast is ready?"

"Mmmm." She yawned again and sat up. "I suppose I better go check it," she groused before climbing down from his lap. While she went to check on the casserole, he dug a brush and a pair of loose shorts out of his pack. After slipping the shorts on, he began the arduous task of brushing the tangles out of his hair.

She peeked at the casserole and shoved it back into the oven. "Not yet," she announced before returning to his side, idly watching him brush his hair. "Why did you put those on?" she asked, gesturing at his soft shorts.

He shrugged. "It just seemed the thing to do. You were dressed. I thought you would be more comfortable if I had on something."

"I had to go out to the spring house to get breakfast," she explained wryly. "It's a good thing I was dressed because when I came back, Llyon was waiting for me on the back porch."

"I can see how that might have been a touch uncomfortable." He set the brush down and swiftly braided his hair in one plait that hung down his back. "Anyway, I don't usually wander around naked, but for you I'll make an exception."

"Oh, you will, huh? Why don't I find a *sharda* for you? Then you can be comfortable with modesty."

"A skirt?" He planted his hands on his hips and frowned at her.

She smiled and pointed out quietly, "You'll need to adjust to wearing one before we bond. Why wait?"

"I don't have one."

"Papa sent a couple of Tyger's new ones out yesterday afternoon. I'll give them to you now and then you'll have them when you're ready," she suggested mildly. She went to the cupboard in the corner and came back with a pile of folded fabric. After pushing them into his unwilling hands, she walked back into the kitchen to check their breakfast.

"A skirt," he muttered with disgust before dropping them on top of his open pack. "I'm glad Trav won't be here to see this…"

# Chapter Nine

**ဢ**

Three days later when Eppie's time ran out with jarring abruptness, the shocking urgency of *schalzina* caught Dancer off balance after spending the intervening days with Eppie in leisurely exploration of the valley around her cabin and the village.

Merlyn had taken the morning to show him around the village, introducing him to the villagers as they encountered them and answering his questions. The *packits* padded along behind them, acting exactly like they were intently listening to the conversation. Finally, nervously, Dancer nodded toward the two animals and asked, "Why are they following us? They look like they're eavesdropping."

"Probably because they are," Merlyn replied mildly. "*Packits* are sentient creatures. If they choose, they can mind talk with you." He smiled at Dancer's shocked face. "On the oldest part of the Talking Wall, they are one of the listed sacred beings, with the charge to protect and revere them. There's a long tradition of some individuals adopting particularly talented young men and serving as advisors and guides."

"Stop." Dancer plopped down on the bench in front of the bakery dome and crossed his arms, hugging his chest. "Just stop a minute. What exactly is a Talking Wall?"

With a soft laugh, Merlyn joined him on the bench and stretched his long legs out in front of him. "The Talking Wall is an enormous hanging wall, about sixty feet high and maybe a hundred feet long. It's a good three-day walk from here at the other end of the valley. Small glyphs the size of my palm are inscribed over the entire surface. It contains history, laws and instructions for living. At the moment, less than a third of it has been translated, so we don't know what other information it may contain. Dai and I have been hoping that there's something on there that explains the passages into the caves from the out-valley. There's a whole raft of archivists that do nothing else except work on the wall."

"And the *packits* are listed on the wall?"

"Uh-hmm. *Packits, dintis, firkas* and *drangs*...though Dai has never seen a *drang* and he thinks they're probably extinct."

Dancer sighed deeply, pinched the bridge of his nose and asked, even as he knew he shouldn't, "What is a *drang*? And those other two things you mentioned?"

Merlyn grinned at Dancer's obvious frustration, remembering his own incredulity when he and Jade had arrived in the valley. With a certain amount of anticipation, he relished Dancer's reaction as he elaborated, "*Dintis* resemble very large, very long-haired dogs. Their older females occasionally adopt a promising young lady. Twice a year they present themselves to the *dinti* keeper and shearer to get their hair cut. The hair is carefully preserved and used in the bonding blankets Tyger weaves." He paused when a vague choking sound escaped Dancer, then, after a moment he continued, "*Firkas* look sort of like gerbils or hamsters. Eppie has a family of *firkas* living in her garden, so if you see something that looks like a mouse, don't kill it. Most gardens have *firkas*. They eat garden pests and certain weeds, but once you tell them a plant is off limits, they never touch it."

Dancer bent over and moaned.

Chuckling, Merlyn just patted his back. "Now *drangs* are an entirely different thing. They're small dragons. According to the Wall, a *drang* will appear and adopt an individual who is exceptionally important to the valley, serving as a mentor for the rest of that individual's life. No one in the valley has seen a *drang* in living memory, so..."

"They're extinct, or there hasn't been anyone important enough for a *drang*," Dancer concluded sourly. "Maybe you can answer another question for me... Why does Eppie have a small dragon identical to mine on her left shoulder? She's named Epona for the horse goddess. Why not a horse?"

Merlyn shrugged lightly. "One day when she was about six, she came to her mother and me and announced that she needed a dragon on her shoulder. We were not amused and worked hard to dissuade her, but two weeks later Dai backed her up. He told us it would be important for her future."

"So that was it? You just gave up and said okay?"

"Exactly." Merlyn leaned a little closer and asked, "Now, would you like to see Tyger's workshop before we go back home?"

Dancer clapped a curled palm over his mouth as a mighty yawn took him by surprise. His eyes filled with tears that he blinked away before unfolding his weary body from the bench. Until he came to the valley, he had been under the mistaken impression that he was in good physical shape, but three days of walking *everywhere* had disabused him of that notion. Waving a hand in front of him, he said, "After you. I've been curious about what Tyger does."

"The tapestry in our front hall was his first masterwork. He weaves most of the fabric used for clothing in the valley, but his great love is working on the bonding and pledging coverlets. The first ones he made were for Eppie." Merlyn turned down a narrow alleyway between two neat yards and led him to a two-story dome with large windows set around the top floor.

Glancing around, Dancer realized that it was the only two-story dome in the village. Curiosity nudged him forward. "This is Tyger's workshop?"

"Yeah. The dome was *our* masterwork," Merlyn declared proudly. "Devising the supports and positioning for the windows, helping Alric design the rollers to make the glass windows and finally hauling in the roof supports..." He sighed in remembered appreciation of the work involved. "We sent Tyger and Llyon down to Talking Wall for an entire moon while we built it. Then, on their birthday they came home just as we finished it."

"For *their* birthday?"

"Llyon has an office, stillroom and library in the back," Merlyn explained with pleasure. "He's nearly finished his healer apprenticeship with Dai. Dai says he's going to be a master healer. We haven't had a master healer in the valley in more than forty years." He pushed the wide door open and motioned Dancer in ahead of him. "Come on in."

The steady clacking of the shuttles and loom masked their entrance so that Dancer got a first glimpse of Tyger absorbed in his work unaware of their presence. The loom was gigantic, fashioned from glittering black *malzhal* wood smoothed to a satiny finish and Dancer realized immediately that the front of the dome was one large open room soaring up to a high cupped roof. Light poured in from the windows circling the second level. Different sized looms filled the lower level, each positioned for maximum use of space. Curved shelving around the walls overflowed with baskets of colored yarns and unspun wool. Next to the door, a large tilted desk similar to a drafting table held a collection of drawings, with a shelf full of what appeared to be hand bound books above the desk. Everything was painfully neat and clean.

With a light mental touch, Merlyn let Tyger know they were there. He turned immediately with a smile, halting his work and demanded, "Well? What do you think?"

Dancer grinned at his undisguised enthusiasm. "I think it's wonderful. Great shop. Beautiful work." He stared around again. "You're an extremely neat and tidy worker. I would never have envisioned something like this."

Nodding in agreement, Tyger pointed out a couple of high stools. "Have a seat. Papa and the village men did a wonderful job with this building. Llyon and I were overwhelmed when we saw it." He went through a door at the back of the room and they could hear him mumbling and some clatter before he reappeared with a tray of steaming mugs and a plate of scones. "Tea time," he declared with a sigh.

After he served them, he took up his own mug and took a hefty swallow. Dancer winced at the thought of swigging down hot tea that fast and Tyger just smiled at him before commenting, "Mine's gotten cold, but I didn't want to toss it out. So what do you think of our village? Papa's been showing you around?"

Dancer cautiously sipped his steaming tea and then nodded. "It's larger than it appears at first. Very organized and well-kept. I'm impressed."

"Not all of the villages are like ours," Tyger warned. "Lost Market was mostly built after Papa and Mama came to the valley. Most of the villagers are first generation or people who were uncomfortable living in their home villages. Things aren't perfect here, any more than they are out-valley."

"Some of the villages aren't much more than a collection of huts." Merlyn cleared his throat. "Lost Market is both a model and a refuge. Dai's Hamlet is similarly laid out, but not as big. Bell's Corners is just a crossroad where two trails meet. There are six families living there. Goodspeed's Delight is more of a walled family compound. About half of them still live in a type of round tent called a *hurka*. Angus Goodspeed the elder had six children about ninety years ago. As far as I can tell, most of his descendents live in the family compound and it's getting a tad overcrowded even though there are few children now."

Dancer smiled into his mug. "The village names are great. What are some of the others?"

With a low chuckle, Tyger obliged him. "Sunrise, Rebaccah's Promise, Broken Pine and Jump Stag Spring. Not that many."

"Not that many what?" inquired Llyon as he came through the door with his arms loaded down with string bags stuffed with small sealed colorful clay pots.

"Villages. Where are you going with those pots?" Tyger asked curiously.

"I'm taking them back to my stillroom. When Ciara was training her apprentice to make salves and lotions, they made extra so she sent them to me. I'll be glad when Robyn is finally old enough to begin her apprenticeship with Ciara."

"Did she happen to make that stuff I use on my hands?" Tyger demanded eagerly.

"Three pots. I've already put them on the table in our room." He disappeared through a different doorway, reappearing in a few moments with his own mug of tea. Eyeing Dancer's soft t-shirt, jogging shorts and dusty Nikes over his mug, he observed, "No *sharda* and sandals?"

"As much walking as I've done in the last three days, my feet would have been killing me if I had been wearing sandals."

"You do know that eventually those shoes will wear out," Tyger retorted. When he shook his head in disapproval, the *chinkas* binding his braids tinkled like a musical waterfall.

Dancer raised an eyebrow, noting the soft *shardas* the twins wore. Unlike Merlyn's plain hunter green *sharda* and *shera*, theirs were gaudy explosions of color and shapes, though thankfully, their *sheras* were unembellished. He shuddered at the mental picture of the terrible clash if the *sheras* were also patterned. "And by then, hopefully I'll be used to the walking."

Llyon perched on a stool with his heels tucked on the lowest rung and idly inquired, "Where's Eppie?"

"She's with your mother, weeding the back garden. Something about there not being any *firkas* to do the weeding." Dancer shot Merlyn a wry glance. "Until this morning, I thought a *firka* was some type of plant."

"Ahhh. Well, *firkas* don't live in Mama's garden because she might accidentally step on them, so Eppie weeds that one by hand." Llyon placed his mug on Tyger's tray and stood up, stretching carefully. "It was nice to visit, but I have a couple of patients to check on so I'll see you later. Ty, don't wait for me."

Making their own preparations to leave, Dancer and Merlyn collected the remaining mugs and carried the tray to the tiny kitchen off the main room while Tyger went back to his loom, already immersed in the intricate pattern he was weaving.

As they walked back to Merlyn's house, Dancer observed, "It's too bad you didn't think to use all that knowledge to make Eppie a real greenhouse and lab. I would think that it wouldn't require nearly as much effort and it's so difficult for her to work in that hot shed."

Merlyn stopped dead and shot him a startled look. "A greenhouse? Why would she need a greenhouse?"

"Why are her dreams so unimportant?" Dancer shot back with sudden heat. "I don't begrudge Tyger or Llyon that beautiful workshop, but what about *Eppie's* dreams? She's worked for years in a grubby little shed that is either hot and dusty, or cold and drafty, just so she can grow *foltins* and *drackas* for the family. *And no one has even noticed!*"

"But she's been waiting for you so she could be bonded!" Merlyn protested in bafflement.

"What does that have to do with her talents and intelligence? Does it make her less? You of all people I would have expected to appreciate the full spectrum of female abilities. You have Jade as a prime example." Dancer turned away in disgust and stalked down the street, leaving Merlyn staring after him with his mouth open.

Abruptly, he snapped it shut and jogged after Dancer, catching up a few houses from his own. "Wait a moment! Are you saying you don't mind her gardening? You think it's like her job?"

"Mind? Why would I mind? I plan to learn everything I can from her! She can make almost anything grow — or haven't you noticed? Her job? It's a gift! Where do you think your herbs came from? She went out into the forest and brought them back to her garden. What about all the new vegetables and greens you fill your gut with? She developed those, too! What are you, as blind as Jade?" Realizing that his hands were clenched in tight fists, Dancer very deliberately relaxed his fingers and planted his hands on his hips. "Eppie's more than a walking womb just waiting to be filled. If we have a baby, that will be nice, but it isn't the entirety of her existence — or mine — anymore than parenting is the only thing you do," he said impatiently. "Did you stop being a doctor when Eppie was born?"

Frowning, Merlyn shook his head. "No, of course not. I didn't realize she was serious..."

"Then you're either blind or an idiot!"

"Probably both and maybe...just busy," Merlyn admitted reluctantly with a slight smile. "If I promise to rectify the problem while you're in seclusion, will you give me a second chance to redeem myself?"

"Maybe. It will depend on how nice the building is...and once you finish that, you should think about a real pottery dome for Wrenna. I can't believe you haven't fixed her up with a better working space when she produces all the pottery for the entire area. What have you been thinking?"

"Clearly, I'm just a male chauvinist pig," Merlyn replied facetiously. "I promise to also check out Wrenna's shed. What you say about her needs is most likely on target."

With a curt nod, Dancer walked away, satisfied for the moment. Just as Merlyn caught up with him, he remembered to ask about the green and blue birds pecking in the back yards they passed. "What are the weird birds I keep seeing?"

"*Peekies.* They're sort of like chickens, though the meat tastes more like game hen. They lay blue and green speckled eggs which we use just like we would chicken eggs." Merlyn opened the swinging gate and led the way around the house to the garden where they found Eppie still weeding and talking to Jade while she rested under a shady tree, industriously crocheting a small blanket. "We're back," he announced quite unnecessarily.

"How did you find it all, Dancer?" Jade inquired as she finished one row and turned the blanket to begin the next.

"Bigger and better organized than I expected. It's a pretty little village," he admitted. He studied Jade's work and inquired, "What are you working on there?"

With faint mischief, Jade blandly replied, "A baby blanket for the grandchild you're going to give me..."

Refusing to be drawn, Dancer merely nodded and asked, "Eppie, how much longer will you be working on that?"

"Done." Picking up her rush basket, she carried it to the compost pile and dumped it before putting the basket away in the small garden shed. "Are you ready to go back to the cabin?"

"More than ready," he sighed. "When will Dai get here?"

Merlyn pursed his lips, then allowed them to stretch into a gentle smile. "Getting a little anxious?" he teased. "Dai will be here after lunch. You and Eppie should go back and make whatever preparations you need to. Leave your packs by the front door and Wolfe will deliver them to Stonehollow while you do your oath-binding."

"You will stop at the cabin on your way?" Eppie inquired solemnly.

"No. You go to the circle after the nooning rest. We'll join you there once Dai has had a chance to rest and eat a snack."

Eppie went to gently kiss her mother's cheek and then willingly submitted to a brief hug from her Papa. "Then we'll see you later," she whispered, unaccountably feeling her eyes fill with tears.

Merlyn tilted her head back and brushed the tears away with his thumbs. "All will be well, Epona Marie. Dancer cares about you. He is a good man."

"I know," she muttered softly. "I don't know why I'm crying."

"Because suddenly, the next stage of your life is upon you. We wish you great joy. Now go with Dancer and prepare." He nudged her toward Dancer who moved immediately to protectively enfold her in his arms. "Take care of her," he charged the younger man. "She's my firstborn."

"With my life." With three short words, the responsibility for Eppie was transferred from one male to another with no other explanation.

* * * * *

At the cabin, they quickly showered in turn, nervously nibbled at the sandwiches Eppie slapped together and double-checked the packs before setting them at the front door. Eppie went to the linen cupboard and removed the heavy bonding and pledging blankets Tyger had woven in anticipation of this day.

Dancer reluctantly slipped on one of the *shardas* Merlyn had so thoughtfully provided. Following Llyon's explicit instructions, he omitted his underwear and found the lack surprisingly airy. The sandals were a bit tricky, but Eppie helped him with the twining laces and before he was quite ready, it was time to go. Eppie waited patiently for him to indicate his willingness to leave for the circle. They studied each other's faces, looking for some sign that they were going to take this final step together. Abruptly, in unison, they both nodded and turned toward the door.

He took the blankets from her, tucking them under his arm and pulled her to his chest with his free arm. Surrendering with a sigh, she wrapped her arms around his waist and rested her head against him. "We're going to walk out that door, down to the bonding circle and pledge to spend our lives together," he said quietly. "Last call. Is this what you want to do?"

Very slowly, she nodded, rubbing her head against his bare shoulder. "Yes," she replied, her voice muffled against his warm, damp skin. She inhaled, breathing in his scent, which had become so familiar in the past three days. "It's exactly what I want to do."

"Me, too," he admitted, tightening his grip briefly before letting her go with a deep sigh. "Let us get on with it, then. Lead the way, baby."

# Chapter Ten

## ❧

When they reached the bonding circle, Eppie stopped just outside the towering sentinel stones and began to disrobe. Following her example, Dancer unfastened his sandals, kicking them to the side and undid his *sharda*. In moments, they stood together, naked and ready to enter the circle. She led the way to the huge altar stone where they carefully spread the pledging blanket, covering the entire top.

"Now what?" he asked in hushed tones.

"Now we'll climb up and sit in the center," she replied softly. "Place the bonding blanket nearby." Following her directions, he joined her in the center of the stone, dumping the bonding blanket next to them. He sat cross-legged and helped her slip down between his knees with her legs wrapped around his waist. Inevitably, his cock rose to the occasion, rigidly bobbing between their bellies. She scooted forward until they touched from shoulder to groin with her damp pussy folds plastered against his balls.

She reached between them and tightly encircled his insistent erection in her hand. "Yes," she hissed, involuntarily pressing her body closer. He throbbed wildly in her warm palm and fluid beaded on the broad head. She smeared it around the blushing mushroomed cap. More fluid welled up and she swiped it down the shaft tightening her grip. When they were pressed so close together that there was no space from shoulder to groin, she rested her head on his shoulder and whispered, "Now, hold me as tightly as you can and close your eyes. Imagine that your mind is a beautiful jeweled box. Now you're going to open the box. Do you see?"

Abruptly, he clearly heard not just words, but emotions and images and overwhelming physical sensations.

*Do you see what I feel for you? Can you tell how much I need you?*

Sensations bombarded him. He could feel her every heartbeat and the clawing demand for completion. The driving strength of that need nearly leveled him. It called to him in an aching primal urge that he wasn't prepared for, overriding all restraint with the deeply primitive instinct to mate.

*No secrets,* she whispered in his mind. *Are you still willing to pledge?*

He took her mouth ruthlessly, thrusting his tongue to meet hers, angling her head for a better fit. *What do you think?* he taunted fiercely. *You have my hard cock in your hand and my mouth on yours. Does it feel like I'm still willing? Do you think there was ever any choice? Do you still think either of us could walk away?*

She melted against him and only then did he realize that she still harbored reservations about their bonding. *No,* she finally admitted in surrender. *I couldn't walk away now.*

With great reluctance, he ended the kiss and asked, "Now what?" as Merlyn, Dai and her oldest brothers arrived at the edge of the circle.

"Now there are words spoken before our witnesses," she said breathlessly. "A private vow. A pledge that we will be one, sharing heart, mind and body. Do you swear?"

"I swear that we will be one, sharing heart, mind and body," he affirmed with solemn commitment. "What about you, Eppie? Do you swear?"

"I swear that we shall be one, sharing heart, mind and body," she vowed, sealing her vow with a soft kiss. Wrapped in each other's arms, they rested there for precious minutes in the morning sun, sharing an intense silent communication that spoke of need, want and growing desire.

"Are you ready to complete your bonding?" Merlyn's voice intruded softly from the edge of the circle.

Lifting his head, Dancer looked at him with renewed determination. "Oh, yeah, we're ready. If we get any more ready, the main event will be over before it begins. What do we do next?"

"We have witnessed your pledging," Merlyn replied. "The bonding rite is a private one. Normally, we would leave you completely alone at this time. However, since you are new to the valley and Eppie has already begun *schalzina*, we will withdraw for now down to the pool in case you need assistance. Once your bonding is complete, Eppie will let us know and we will leave you alone then."

Dancer shrugged. "If it makes you more comfortable, it's fine with me. The process, as you and Llyon explained it, doesn't seem very difficult."

"Not difficult, no," Llyon corrected. "We merely wish to hedge against the unforeseen."

"Well, whatever you're going to do, get on with it. You're holding up the ceremony," Dancer declared somewhat impatiently. His curt reply evidently convinced them that all was well and they melted away toward the small pool. "Ready, Eppie?" he asked quietly. When she whimpered softly, he ruthlessly suppressed the urge to possess her immediately. He reached with trembling fingers for the small leather pouch at his side. Tugging it open, he removed the tiny, jeweled knife. "Give me your left hand, baby." He took her hand firmly in his.

First he slashed a shallow cut in her palm, then slashed his own. Bright red blood welled up and ran down their wrists. He tossed the knife down and lifted her up on her knees, readying her for the final consummation. Placing their slashed palms together, he vowed clearly, "By the mingling of our blood and this sacrifice, I take this woman for my bond mate until death."

Overwhelming waves of arousal crashed over them. Teeth chattering, Eppie asked, "Why is it always the woman that makes the sacrifice?"

He grasped her hips firmly and grinned. "Bite me, baby," as he brought her down, impaling her with one stroke. After one sharp cry, Eppie feathered kisses down his neck until she reached the smooth muscle of his shoulder. Slowly, she licked the dragon tattoo covering the warm skin with erotic flicks of her tongue. Dancer felt her internal muscles clench tightly on his cock. Abruptly, with no warning, she sank her fangs in the taut shoulder muscle, biting down with ferocious strength.

Heat jolted through Dancer's body with the flash of a forest fire and he slumped against her body, vaguely wondering how he could have had the stupidity to actually tell her to bite him. It was only an *expression*. And then, the darkness roared up like a ravening beast and consumed him.

Eppie sat in his lap, securely anchored with his cock buried in her pussy and struggled to hold him upright. Calling frantically for help, she wrapped her arms around his broad back and held on. Llyon pounded into the clearing, followed more slowly by Tyger.

"What happened?" Ly demanded with consternation.

"He passed out when I bit him," she replied in exasperation. "I can't hold him up much longer. Are you going to help, or are you going to ask questions?"

Shaking his head in self derision, Tyger climbed up onto the stone, sat down against Dancer wedged back-to-back and snarled, "If you ever mention this to me again, I'll tell Mama about the time you sneaked out to go swimming naked with Micah."

"You went swimming naked with Micah?" Llyon demanded. "Why would you do something like that?"

"Because I wanted *some* experience," she replied through gritted teeth, determined that she was going to kill them the first chance available. "Micah was safe because he's *garzhan*.

He was willing for me to practice on him and curious, too. What does that have to do with now?"

"Nothing, actually," Llyon admitted. He hopped up on the stone, checked the bite on Dancer's shoulder, felt his pulse and shrugged. "He seems to be fine. The bite's not bleeding. We'll wait a few minutes and see if he wakes up. I don't recall this ever happening before." He found their bonding blanket, shook it out and draped it over her shoulders. Spying the tiny knife, he slipped it back into its pouch and tossed it over the side onto their pile of clothing. With a sigh, he sat down facing the woods and asked, "You are okay?"

Grinding her teeth in frustration, she snapped, "Define okay. I'm sitting naked in the midst of my oath-binding with my mate unconscious, in the presence of my two brothers. How is this good?"

"Well," Tyger replied thoughtfully, "Papa and Dai could be here, too. They opted to stay away. And unless I'm mistaken, your mate's cock is still hard so you're not in any danger." He felt her shift behind him and warned, "If you hit me, I'll leave and you can hold him up by yourself."

Dancer surfaced about then. "You bit me," he accused Eppie in outrage. "Are you nuts? I was just kidding when I told you to 'bite me'."

"It was necessary to do it while we were joining," she explained calmly. "Without the transformation, you would have eventually died once we completed that. First of course, you would go insane…"

"What? Like a black widow spider? You get what you need and I die?"

"No, of course not," she said impatiently. "Without the missing essential component you can't survive here. My fangs injected the missing enzyme, triggering transformation. I must say your reaction was a bit dramatic."

"Don't ever do anything like that again without discussing it with me first," he commanded very softly. "I'm not a puppet for you to pull my strings. If this bonding is going to work, you'll have to learn to communicate." Tilting her head up with implacable force, he kissed her hard, plundering her mouth and reclaiming his place as dominant protector and defender.

*Well, that was interesting,* Tyger observed silently. *Our new bond-brother isn't a pushover, even if he doesn't react well to bites!*

*No… This binding should be very entertaining. He has a very straightforward way of communicating,* Llyon agreed with droll humor. *I do believe that Eppie has met her match.*

Lifting his head, Dancer rolled his shoulders and pulled the blanket more securely around Eppie. "Don't take this the wrong way, but you two can hit the road now. I'm pretty sure we can manage the rest of this on our own," he said firmly. "Thank you for being here for Eppie."

"Now that must have hurt," Tyger replied mockingly. "Just make sure you don't ever cause her any grief." Ignoring the implied threat, Dancer waited until they were gone before tossing the blanket to the side.

Eppie gasped with relief. "Thank you! I was so hot I thought I was going to melt!" A light breeze moved through the circle, blowing damp strands of their long hair around them.

Dancer carefully brushed the dark wisps away from her face and studied her expression. "I can feel you squeezing my cock to death," he teased quietly. "Did I hurt you?"

Amused, she leaned back a little and looked down to where they were joined. "I don't think so. I was so involved in my duty that I barely felt the tear. And then, you filled me so completely that all I can feel now is stuffed," she confided shyly. "It feels wonderful, but I desperately need you to move it a little."

He immediately thrust in deeper and was rewarded with her appreciative moan. "Like that?" Withdrawing just as far as the *schela* would permit, he paused a second, savoring the extreme pleasure it gave him when it clamped directly beneath the broad head. Then, he thrust again, enjoying the snug tug on his cock as he pushed through the tight ring. "Oh, yeah. Just like that," he said with a rough breath. With her anchored by her death grip on his shoulders, he was free to move his hands to her breasts, tweaking the nipples until they were hard little points. He tugged on them gently. Impulsively, he pressed them together and dipping his head, he flicked his tongue across the sensitive tips.

"Yes!" she cried as the broad, thick head rubbed high against the inner wall of her pussy, kindling the final stages of *schalzina*. The *schela* contracted in waves, clamping down with increasing pressure as Eppie pressed down, grinding her mons against Dancer's groin.

Slowly, he pulled against the clutching compression, reflecting that he would most likely have a sore cock when they were finished, but it would be worth it. Slipping one nipple into his warm mouth, he suckled hard while thrusting his cock in as far as it would go.

She cried out and climaxed with great tugging contractions and unable to prevent it, he joined her, hot spurts of semen surging out to fill her. As they clung together, struggling for breath, blinding flashes of lightning crackled around the circle, flashing from stone to stone. A flickering beam lashed their palms before crashing into the stone beneath them. Thunder crashed all around them as the stones lit up in a weird bluish light and then a deathly silence fell over the circle. Dancer gathered Eppie closer to him.

On the path to Eppie's cabin, Merlyn, Dai, Tyger and Llyon halted and stared at each other in astonishment. The ancient tales of oath-bindings that ended in such a display were the stuff of legend. Until now. Merlyn laughed out loud. "Something tells me the valley is very pleased with their bonding. Hurry! After that extraordinary display, there's going to be a hell of a storm."

"Should we check on them?" Llyon inquired tentatively.

"No. I've told Eppie to move quickly for cover. They should be fine if they go straight to Stonehollow."

In the circle, Dancer cuddled Eppie close and enunciated very slowly, "What the hell was that?"

"Papa says that the valley is pleased with our bonding and that we need to get to Stonehollow as soon as possible. He says there's going to be a big storm after that oath-binding!" A cold wet wind sprang up, howling around the circle. Eppie was shivering and her teeth were chattering.

Lifting Eppie from his lap, he settled her on the blanket. Wearily, he staggered to his feet and then helped her to stand up. With one accord, they climbed down from the stone and dressed, moving with desperate haste. Overhead black thunderheads billowed and lightning crackled as she helped him wrap his *sharda* around his waist. He yanked the coverlets from the stone and followed her down the path past the waterfall.

On the way to Stonehollow, Eppie stumbled, nearly pulling Dancer down with her. Whatever constraints had been in place were gone, leaving them with the starkly primal urge to mate. It seemed not to matter at all that they had just finished. Eppie desperately needed his hard thick cock filling the empty place inside her. Suddenly the cold rain poured down out of a stormy sky. Treetops whipped and bent in the wind. He felt her belly clench with tension.

Standing in the middle of the path, he wildly searched for shelter. Spying a dry area beneath a huge broad-leafed tree, he urged Eppie under the temporary safety of the wide branches. Hastily he spread their bonding blanket. Slumping down, he ripped the *sharda* open, leaned back against the huge trunk and grasping her by the waist, lifted her above him and brought her down, impaling her with one stroke.

Immediately, they both exploded, shaking with the strength of their completion. She cried out. He felt another climax ripple through her, gently titillating his hard shaft.

Another involuntary thrust triggered his second climax. She screamed softly as she tightened her thighs and then another orgasm swamped her. The wind flung a cold blast of rain at their heads and shoulders, lashing their unbound hair around them.

She rested her head on his shoulder, exhausted with the violence of her orgasm, yet already aroused again beyond bearing. Involuntarily, the *schela* tightened around him and she reveled in the feeling of his hot, hard cock, stretching her, filling her completely. He braced under the onslaught of her ever-renewing hunger stunned by the creeping awareness that this wasn't a mild case of *schalzina*, but rather the more severe sexual fury of *schalzah* that he was dealing with. "Dancer!" she whispered frantically, shivering with need.

"Shh. We're going to be fine. Hang on as tight as you can, honey." He hoisted her hips closer and thrust with deep, sure strokes until he felt the unraveling that heralded another release. Time passed unheeded as he struggled to cope with their spiraling, unrelenting needs. Hours later, deep in the night, she collapsed against his chest, her body slack and boneless with complete satiety as the last echoing tremors of *schalzah* faded.

After a long while, moving with aching slowness, he climbed to his feet, hoisted her in his arms and carried her the rest of the way to Stonehollow. Later, neither of them had a clear idea how they had reached the bonding cottage. The next coherent memory they had was their stumbling struggle to reach the soft rug before the dying fire flickering in the fireplace. Trembling with fatigue, he pulled their bonding blankets over them before they fell asleep with his cock snugly buried again in her still throbbing pussy.

# Chapter Eleven

80

The bonding storm lashed the trees and domes in Lost Market. As the storm's fury increased and darkness fell, Llyon's anxiety grew. Tyger never worked this late. He had been a little annoyed at losing their wager over the *sharda*, declaring that it was twice as irritating that the *sharda* Dancer wore one of *his!* Llyon knew his twin very well. He tended to deal poorly when things didn't go his way. Finally, he had stalked out to work off his aggravation in his workshop.

Though Llyon was ready for bed, with his hair released from the confining braids and only his house *sharda* on, he suddenly anchored the bright red strands back with a large comb, slipped on a *woolie shera* against the storm and went out to the workroom in search of Tyger. He could feel Ty's terrible pain and anguish. Llyon suspected that Tyger was suffering from a very rare form of mind frenzy—*schalzintelo*—and clearly he didn't retain enough sanity to seek out his bond mate.

It was time to end it by taking on the commitment of a covenant bond with Tyger. From the time they were six they had known that their twin-bond set them apart from other twin sibs. The twin-bond tied their lives inextricably, binding them mind, body and soul. They were bound so closely that the moment one of them died, so would the other. Sibs with the twin-bond cemented that relationship via the covenant bond. And without the final commitment of the covenant bond, Llyon wouldn't be able to help him. That would require the deep mental bond of *rapport*.

Minutes later, Llyon stood rooted in the shadowy workroom, stunned at the total destruction. Tyger's towering giant loom was reduced to a shambles of small chunks of *malzhal* wood. For long moments he stood there frozen, unable to think, unable to comprehend what could have possibly happened. Thunder crashed overhead and jagged flashes of light threw the chaos into sharp relief. A mournful keening cry lifted the skin on his neck and suddenly he knew with paralyzing certainty that Tyger had done this. Tyger had destroyed his great loom! He turned and ran out into the storm with terror in his chest.

Heart in mouth, Llyon pounded across the wild river meadow toward the lake as fast as his long legs would carry him. Rain poured down in the darkness, hiding his brother from view, but he ran with the deep conviction of the twin-bond. Tyger's grief and pain burst free sending him on frenzied race to the lake tonight to end it. In the heart of the storm, his keening call rose like the anguished howl of a *wolvala*, above the drumming of the rain.

As he ran, Llyon stripped off his clothing, leaving it strewn in his wake. He saw Tyger slowly walking into the cold, dark water, his bright hair spread around him. His clothing and precious hair *chinkas* were carelessly dumped on the sand. With all the yearning and anguish he felt deep in his soul, Llyon cried out, "Ty! Wait! Please don't leave me alone!"

Tyger turned to face him. Lightning flickered and Llyon could see the frantic despair on his face. Reaching up, Ly yanked out the comb holding his hair back from his face so that it streamed down around him as he ran, covering him to below the hip line. "I offer a covenant!" he shouted into the wind. Tyger, standing naked knee-deep in the lake, was shocked into immobility. "Please don't leave me, Ty. Please, I beg you... I offer you the covenant!"

Tyger stared at his brother with astonished comprehension as a tidal wave of agony overwhelmed him and he went to his knees clutching his head against the pain. "Llyon," he groaned. "You can't do this..."

Heedlessly, Llyon splashed into the cold lake until he reached his brother. Hauling him to his feet, he jerked him into a tight embrace. "Shh. Just let me hold you. I can help." It took superhuman strength to hold Tyger upright when he sagged as the next wave of pain struck.

He groaned. "I hurt so damned much, Ly," he admitted through gritted teeth. "Help me," he pleaded.

Llyon cupped Tyger's face in his warm hands. "You only had to ask. You know it's past time! Tell me. Tell me you will accept the covenant!"

With shaking hands, Ty gripped his shoulders as he stared deep into Llyon's eyes. "Llyon!" he groaned. "I don't want to tie you to me that way. What if you decide someday that you want a bond mate and children?" Tears rolled down his cheeks, mingling with the rain.

"You're an idiot, Ty. This has always been our destiny. We will abide by the fate sent to us. Perhaps we will one day find a woman to share," Llyon insisted calmly. "Come with me, out of this storm before we're struck by lightning. We have waited for *rapport* long enough!" Light flashed across the sky, illuminating the beach and the two young men staggering toward the old stone lake house.

At home in Lost Market, Merlyn woke with the sudden certainty that an important change had come to the valley. He ached with exhaustion, positive that he hadn't been asleep very long. The storm whipped up from their daughter's bonding rite had pushed Jade into one of the most intense string of *schalzina* episodes of their life. Normally, he reveled in fulfilling her needs in *schalzina*, but tonight, her urgency had threatened to drag them into the fury of *schalzah*. He could only grimly hold on and pray for the *schalzina* to run its course before that happened. She was asleep, at last, breathing slowly as one deeply exhausted. As he stirred, moving carefully so that he wouldn't wake her, he heard Dai's calm voice in his mind. *Merlyn.*

*What's wrong?*

He felt Dai sigh. *I must talk to you about Llyon and Tyger…*

Somehow, Merlyn got the notion that it wasn't going to be a comfortable talk. *They're all right?*

*They swore a covenant bond tonight.*

Merlyn froze, even forgetting to breathe. *What? Why?*

*Tyger was going to commit suicide,* Dai replied flatly. *He tried to hide it from Llyon, but Llyon caught him at the lake and offered him the covenant.*

Mentally, Merlyn floundered, trying to come to grips with the implications. *Tyger accepted? He never gave any indication…*

*Tonight, he was pushed into schalzintelo from the bonding storm.* He could almost feel Dai's grim smile. *We've always been aware that they would need to swear a covenant bond because of their twin-bond anyway,* Dai replied impatiently. *It's possible that one or both of them might bond with a woman in the future. Perhaps, they will even share a woman… But if not, then so be it. You and I discussed this possibility. This wasn't a sacrifice, or a seduction, but a complete sharing.* He sighed again. *I warned you I thought this was inevitable – and when it was necessary for Tyger's sanity, Llyon showed no hesitation. They needed the power of* rapport *The mental bond will allow them to support each other. You know very well that Llyon would have followed him even into death because of their twin-bond.*

*What should we do now?* Merlyn asked, bewildered.

*Nothing. They're grown men, not little boys and they're old enough to finally make this decision,* Dai suggested curtly. *They're at the lake house. That is a good, safe place for them. No one will intrude there after this storm. The meadow will be a shallow lake for several days. Once the water's gone down, they'll seal their bond in the circle, but just like any other bonding couple, they'll need some time alone to cement the covenant relationship. Since that damned lake house is freezing, I suggest that you figure out how to keep them warm and fed. Above all, leave them alone. When they're ready, they'll come home.*

Jade stirred sleepily, missing the physical connection with Merlyn on some deep mysterious level. After more than twenty years of usually sleeping intimately joined, the sudden emptiness left her bereft. *Merlyn?*

*Shh. Go back to sleep.* Climbing back in the gently swinging bed, he shifted around until he was comfortably hilted deep in her snug pussy. Rippling contractions played over his sensitive cock. Gently, he pressed deeper and she rewarded him with another undulating squeeze as a distant echo of the *schalzina* seeped through her.

*Mmmm. Still hurting, huh?* His hand stole to the closest nipple, tweaking it gently.

*Only a little. Have I exhausted you beyond all reason?*

*Not yet.*

*Then, come to me…* She tugged at him, until he was stretched out between her bent knees, resting his chest lightly on her soft breasts.

*Better?* he inquired, plunging deeper. Retreating as she stifled a gasp, he plunged again until he felt her womb tickling the head. The *schela* gripped his cock just below the flaring head, holding him deep and preventing him from withdrawing. Plunging deeper, he willingly followed her over the edge, drenching her womb with his seed. "I love you, Jade."

He held her close as he rolled over so that she draped bonelessly on his chest. Drowsing contentedly in the aftermath, they lay quietly enjoying the soft hidden convulsions that continued long afterward as they were locked together.

"Why were you awake?"

"I was talking to Dai."

"In the middle of the night? What's happened?"

"Llyon and Tyger swore covenant. They will have their bonding in a few days."

"Ohhh." She was still, thinking for a while. "Why now?"

"Tyger tried to suicide. The bonding storm plunged him into *schalzah*. I didn't realize he was in that much pain. Thankfully, Llyon caught him in time. We would have lost both of them." He sighed. "They're bonding at the house near the lake. Dai said to leave them alone until they're ready to come home." He reached up to brush her bright soft curls back from her face. "We need to fix them a separate compartment in the compound because they're going to definitely need privacy even when they come home."

"Give them Eppie's cabin. By the time Dancer and Eppie finish their seclusion, we'll have the boys' compartment renovated for them."

"As usual, my love, you've got it all figured out. I believe that I'll keep you, even if you do nearly wear me out with your insatiable lusts."

"Uh-huh. You never complained before. Maybe you're getting old?" She yawned widely. "It's cold at the lake house. Shouldn't we take them some blankets and stuff?"

He yawned. "Tomorrow we'll figure it out. I expect that Arturo or Wolfe will be happy to cart some supplies out there for them. For now—I'm getting old and need my sleep."

\* \* \* \* \*

As the storm rumbled across the valley, bond mates in villages and settlements from one end to the other inexplicably launched into *schalzina*. Rain poured down, lightning flashed and thunder crashed in the most prolonged storm in memory.

While everyone else was safely inside, Silence Brown huddled naked at the base of Needle Rock as the storm crashed all around her. She wept in despair, knowing that *he* was out there, just waiting for the storm to end. Her shorn blonde hair curled damply around her face. She had to get away before *he* killed her. Life with him had been an achingly empty and debasing nightmare, but now, something had finally snapped in his mind. He blamed her for his inability to do *something*—and he was determined that she would pay for it. He had shaken his limp *kzusha* at her, screaming that it was all her fault, but she couldn't quite figure out how that could be.

When the bonding storm struck and he still wasn't able to control his body, he had tied her to the bed and whipped her in a wild frenzy until her back and buttocks bled. Then he had seized her by her hair, dragging her to the kitchen table, where he slashed at the blonde strands with her biggest knife. When the last strand was severed, it freed her for the few seconds she needed to escape. But she had seen him in the lightning strike, stalking her with the knife still in his hand. Where could she hide?

Thunder cracked overhead and the sky lit up, revealing Homer standing naked less than ten feet away. He raised his arms above him and screamed into the storm, though she couldn't understand what he said. Suddenly, a flashing bolt shot down, melding with the knife. He seemed to light up within as though he was burning, then with a final crash of thunder, he dropped flat on his face and was still.

Trembling, she got to her feet and slowly edged up to Homer's body. When he didn't move, she nudged him with her toe. He lay there like a cold lump of dough, flaccid and heavy. Frantically, she peered around her, wondering what to do. Where should she go?

As the rain continued to fall in a heavy silver curtain, a man appeared out of the tempest and tenderly wrapped a blanket around her. "Silence, come with me!" he commanded firmly. "Come. We must get out of the storm!"

"Arano! I don't know what to do! I think Homer's dead!"

"Leave him. My father and I will take care of him. Come with me. I'll walk you home." Arano led her down the path to her dome, overcoming her resistance to returning there. "I will send someone to stay with you," he promised. "Tomorrow, my father will talk to you about the death rites. Try to sleep tonight."

She stopped and turned to face him. "I didn't do anything, Arano. I swear I didn't do anything to him." She picked at the wet ragged strands of hair plastered across her face. "He chopped my hair off with my kitchen knife!"

He pushed the hair back from her face. "Silence! I believe you. Trust me. I will take care of everything. Now, go inside and get dried off." When she didn't move, he gave her a gentle push. "Go. I have to go fetch my father." He watched to make sure she was safely inside before he ran down the path back to the village. There was much to do before daylight. And once this was all settled, Silence would finally belong to him.

In the early dawn light, Dai and Arano stood studying the body, shoulders hunched as the rain poured down, though the wind no longer whistled through the village. Homer was despised by all who knew him and a personal puzzle to Dai. He had never been able to figure out why his daughter, Silence had run away with Homer when she was a very young woman. Staring down at the pudgy corpse, he couldn't find it in his heart to grieve in any way for the man.

"What happened?" he wearily inquired.

Arano visibly straightened and braced himself. "He was chasing Silence with a knife. She told me that he became angry, attacked her and chopped all her hair off with one of her kitchen knives." He gestured to the foot of Needle Rock. "She was crouched down there. As he approached her with the knife held above his head, a lightning bolt hit the knife, traveled down through his body and scorched the ground there," he pointed at a blackened patch near Homer's bare feet.

His shoulders moved in a light shrug. "I was awake and heard the lightning crack. I came to see if anything was damaged and found her here. So, I walked her home, thinking I would wake Papa." He shot a questioning glance at Dai. "By the time I had escorted her home, I knew you were still in the village so I came back here to meet you."

Dai answered his unspoken question with one sentence. "Tyger and Llyon swore a covenant bond in the middle of the night."

"Ah." Arano nodded soberly.

"I am here to serve as a witness to the bond and enter it into the records." Dai nudged Homer's arm. "I suggest we drag this carrion up to the top of Needle Rock. Since the valley has spoken so clearly, I suspect it will also dispose of him, too."

Arano nodded again in silent agreement. "I brought an old sheet as that was my assessment, also. Time grows short if we are to move him before the villagers start stirring."

Dai helped him roll Homer onto the sheet and then they dragged him up the trail to the peak of Needle Rock where they dumped him in the center of the flat summit. "I can't truthfully say that I'm sorry about this man's death."

Arano carefully considered his next words before informing Dai, "He was beating her, Dai. He was not a worthy man. Do not feel guilty because of the feelings in your heart. His death was just."

Slow tears rolled down Dai's face. "You know this for truth?"

"I do. She bears his marks on her back. Wrenna had gone to care for her." Arano stared out at the heavy silver rain. "I had thought to send Llyon, but I couldn't find him. I didn't know that he would not be available." He turned and met Dai's eyes. "I believe that they were never truly bonded. Homer never changed, Dai...not even after all the years he was here. No fangs, no blue skin, no pointed ears. I was curious and asked around, but I could find no one who claimed to be his *semtorn* and no one who witnessed their oath-binding. When I questioned Silence about it, she seemed to not understand what I was asking. Nor did she seem to understand why he was so angry, but I believe he went insane because he couldn't get erect. Without the enzyme, that would happen not long after entering the valley."

Staring down at the body sprawled on the ground, Dai shook his head slowly. "You might be correct. Silence left me before she had the required classes... I will go to my daughter and try to make amends. Thank you for your gentle care. Now, let us go down from here so that the valley may finish its work."

As they trudged down the trail, a flash of light lit up the village and Needle Rock trembled. They hesitated briefly and then continued down as Dai observed, "It is done."

# Chapter Twelve

∞

Dancer woke abruptly, shivering as cool air crept across his face. He lay there, motionless as he silently studied their surroundings. The fire had burned out, leaving a pile of cold ashes in the fireplace. Cold gray light crept around the edges of the window covers. The high bed across the room beckoned with the promise of warmth and soft comfort, but he ruefully acknowledged that they weren't likely to sample it any time soon. Deep within the warm depths of her silky pussy, Eppie had a firm grasp on his cock and until she released him, they wouldn't be moving.

According to the detailed information Merlyn had imparted during his explanations the morning just prior to their oath-binding, Eppie had no control over their locking. Involuntarily, Dancer grinned when he envisioned explaining his predicament to his brother. Trav would never believe it.

"What's so funny?" Eppie asked in a soft mutter as she burrowed closer to his warm chest. Clutching their bonding blanket closer against her breasts, she tilted her head back so that she could see Dancer's face.

He slipped one hand around so that he cupped her breast, noting the hard nipple pressing into his warm palm. "Cold?" he queried teasingly. "I was just thinking that we would be warmer up in the bed."

She yawned sleepily. "So why don't we move?"

He softly nuzzled her ear. "That will be a tad difficult until you relax that death grip you have on my poor abused cock," he pointed out.

Her entire body grew still as awareness settled within her. "Oh-h."

"Uh-hum. *Oh-h*. I don't think I'm quite up to hauling us both up onto that bed from this position. If we were face to face, I might have a chance, but..." he trailed off with a slight gasp when the muscles in her pussy tightened around his cock.

"Sorry," she muttered. "I can't seem to control it."

"No problem," he assured her breathlessly. "I love a tight kitty." Another squeeze broke the little control he possessed and he pressed his hips against her soft warm ass, burying the broad head of his cock against her womb. "I *really* love a tight pussy," he reiterated with a deep breath.

She moaned and tightened around him. "I'm glad I make you happy," she wheezed out between whimpers.

"I have to tell you that I've never fucked like this where I couldn't move," he panted next to her ear.

"Hmmm. I guess that means that you'll just have to get creative."

"Creative." He slowly inched back until the head of his cock was caught up in her locking ring, then shoved forward with enthusiasm. She shrieked. "Was that what you had in mind, baby?" he whispered in her ear as he withdrew again to the *schela*. He felt her pleasure roll through him, combining with his own.

"Oh, yes," she moaned as he swiftly pushed forward again.

The small aborted movements drove the nerves in his cock head crazy while also forcing him to glide across her G-spot. She inhaled sharply and shuddered as the combined sensations flashed through her. In a much shorter time than he normally took, he felt the first streaks of his climax. He struggled to hold back until Eppie was ready, but once he felt the ripples of her orgasm, he lost all control, shooting his seed deep against the opening to her womb in pulse after hot pulse.

He felt tiny sucking motions against the head as though her cervix was milking him. Then, very slowly she relaxed around him, allowing him to withdraw.

He turned her to face him and cuddled her in his arms. "What was that?" he asked quietly. "It felt like you were nibbling on me like a kissing fish."

"That's the *mhital*. Papa and Llyon think that it ensures pregnancy. Between the *schela* and *mhital*, you're locked in the best position..." she trailed off, studying his face. "You understand that here in the valley, a man's primary responsibility is impregnating his mate and caring for her and his children?"

He kissed her gently. "Both your papa and Llyon explained that. I just wasn't aware of how your body was designed to help out. It's a very strange sensation. Very erotic."

"Oh. You're not upset?" she asked softly. She knew there were so many adjustments he would need to deal with here in the valley. On this, his fifth day, he had faced pledging, oath binding, *schalzah* and a new bond mate with surprising grace. "I know there are many changes for you. When I dreamed about it, I didn't think we would be bonded so quickly."

"You planned for a little more assimilation time, huh?" He lifted his hand and tenderly brushed dark silky strands back from her face. "I think I was catching some of your *schalzina*, even before our pledging. I couldn't have waited, Eppie. I needed you too much." Suddenly he grinned. "We'll cope just fine. I'll be so stunned most of the time, I won't know what hit me until we're old and gray."

She pursed her lips in thought. "Somehow, I don't believe that you stun easily. I think you are very seldom caught off guard, my bond mate." Sighing deeply, she rolled onto her back and gingerly stretched. "Do you suppose we should get up? I need a bath and something to eat." She shivered with cold. "And a fire."

"All right." Dancer climbed to his feet and stretched weary, aching muscles while she admired the view. "Fire. Bath. Breakfast. I should be able to manage that before I drag you off to bed." He smiled down at her, noting her keen interest in his body. "Of course, if you keep staring at my cock like that, we'll have to skip the bath and breakfast," he observed mildly.

She jerked her gaze away and rolled to her feet with a groan. "No, no. I definitely need a hot soak in the tub." Sliding him a sly look, she added, "But the tub is big enough for two..." before she ran for the bathing room.

"Witch!" While he built a fire to warm the cottage, he listened as she hummed tunelessly while she prepared the bath. Shaking his head mournfully, he thought what a pity it was that he was bonded to a woman who couldn't carry a tune in a basket. Fortunately, he'd discovered she had other qualities he was much more interested in...

Their bath became a leisurely exploration of each other's bodies, a time for touching and feeling that had been denied to them the previous day by the urgency of *schalzah*. At last, reluctantly, she sighed and admitted, "Much as I'm enjoying this, we really need to eat."

Dancer slipped his fingers between her legs and tenderly petted the puffy folds. "Hmm. I suppose so. I love the way you're bare down here." He frowned at the pink tinged rash across her breasts. "I've scratched you." When he brushed his hand across his chin, he felt spots he'd missed with the blue cream. "Do you have a pot of that hair remover here?"

She arched an eyebrow in inquiry. "Of course. Why?"

"I missed a few spots last time. I guess I wasn't paying attention to what I was doing," he teased gently. "Somebody distracted me from the usual careful job I do when I shave."

"Shave? What's that?" she asked with bright curiosity.

"Shaving is a barbaric custom involving the scraping of whiskers or hair from various body parts with a sharp blade," he informed her as he slipped a gentle finger in her slick pussy. "Most men must shave their faces every day. Women have an even tougher time as they shave under their arms, their legs and some of them even shave their pussies."

"That *is* barbaric," she declared with disgust. She pointed out a small pottery pot with a green glyph on the side. "If you hand me that pot, I think I can provide you with a better solution." He retrieved the pot and watched while she removed the lid to reveal the blue-colored salve. She dipped a couple of fingers in, smearing the dollop over his whiskers. He felt a faint tingling. Then she wiped his face clean with a washcloth. He glided his fingers over his chin, noting the smooth, soft whisker-free skin.

"Do you use that blue salve on your pussy?"

She tilted her head back so that she could see his face and frowned. "Yes...why?"

"I don't want anything between you and my mouth when I get around to eating you again like a yummy dessert." He leaned closer, amused by her stunned expression and whispered in her ear, "You have no idea how much I'm looking forward to tasting you again."

"No," she admitted with a little moan as the memory of his caresses flashed across her mind. She clambered to her feet and stepped from the tub. Slowly drying off, she turned to face him with a secret smile on her face. "I'm looking forward to it. So that we don't waste any more time, I'll go start preparing real food for us to eat." Dropping the bath sheet on a hook, she slipped out of the bathing room, still naked.

With a thoughtful expression on his face, Dancer emptied the tub and dried off. She seemed to be very comfortable with her nudity. He tried in vain to imagine what this courtship would have been like out-valley. For sure, he liked the brevity of the 'ceremony' compared to the last wedding he'd attended. Following her example, he strolled into the main room naked. "I didn't think much about it yesterday, but what are we supposed to do about clothing when we get around to dressing?"

He heard a small clicking sound just before a tiny flame puffed up from the stove. Curious and distracted, he watched her place several pale gray rocks around the flame. "What are those?"

"Hot rocks. Papa says that they are similar to your charcoal, but they burn longer, can be extinguished with water and once they dry out they can be reused." She unwound a paper-wrapped bundle revealing a chunk of rare meat. Competently slicing several thick pieces from it with a wickedly sharp knife, she slapped them onto a flat griddle and set them over the fire. "How hungry are you?"

"The last thing I ate was cheese on a fresh roll yesterday morning and I think I had maybe three or four bites of lunch. I was too nervous to eat then. For some reason, I seem to be starving," he teased with a grin.

She shot him a look of pure innocence. "So *rowan* slices, *peekie* eggs and toasted bread slices with *quoltania* jam should hold you until lunch." She lifted down a beautiful deep blue pottery bowl from the shelf above the sink and selected four green eggs from it.

"I'm sure it will all be delicious, but exactly what are *rowan* slices and *quoltania* jam? I've never found a good time to ask..." he inquired over his shoulder as he moved to the fireplace to check his fire.

She flashed him a quick smile. "I have a dictionary for you. Papa and Mama helped me with it. If you look on the mantle, you'll see some sheets of *linual* there."

"*Linual*?"

"Hmm. Paper? I *think* that's what Mama called it." She grinned. "When Arano told us you were coming, Papa and Mama thought it would be easier if you could check the list on your own. I didn't realize how different things were. It seemed like a very long list." Sliding the hot *rowan* slices to the edge of the griddle, she broke the eggs in the center and tossed the shells into a small basket on the counter. Setting a round loaf on the heavy wood counter, she rapidly sliced off four rounds, before quirking an eyebrow at him. "How many pieces of bread do you want?"

Dance looked up from the stack of sheets he was studying and eyed the pile of slices. "How many of those are yours?"

"Two."

"Cut a couple more," he decided absently. He tapped the *linual* sheets with one finger. "This was a very good idea, love. You said before that Arano told you I was coming. How much does Arano see?"

Eppie turned away from him and served the eggs and *rowan* slices on two light blue pottery platters. Tossing the bread slices onto the griddle, she arranged them in two rows, fussing with them while she considered what to tell Dancer.

"Eppie? I think I would like an answer now." His implacable tone convinced her that the truth was the only answer he would accept. Already, she knew enough about him to realize that he would be relentless when he was seeking answers.

Shrugging lightly in surrender, she turned to face him. "Arano frequently has visions. He sees things that are going to happen." Turning away again, she located the short squat pot of *quoltania* jam and placed it on the table.

"He sees the future? That must suck for him." Dancer set aside the *linual* sheets and rummaged through the drawers until he located eating utensils and napkins. Setting two places, he searched for something to drink. "What do we have to drink?"

"Water, herbal tea, *rowan* milk…"

"Water." His firm reply amused her. She heard the shudder in his voice when he added, "I don't think I'm ready for *rowan* milk."

She speared the bread slices with a fork and added them to the platters. Setting them in place, she disappeared into the bathing room and returned with two small bathing sheets. With a small smile, she placed one on each of the chair seats. "Seats are too cold for bare bottoms," she said succinctly.

"If you sat on my lap, I bet I could keep your bottom warm," he offered innocently.

"I bet you could," she agreed with a soft laugh. "But I like my food hot and I have a notion that by the time I got to eat my breakfast, it would be cold."

"Anyone ever tell you that you're picky?" he inquired with interest, watching her spread the blue *quoltania* jam meticulously on her toast.

"I don't think so."

"Hmph. You never gave me an answer about clothes. It seems that I remember your dad saying something about Wolfe bringing our packs over her... And now that I think about it, where did the food come from?" After a cautious taste of the meat and eggs, he devoured them with a hearty appetite. Not bad — not bad at all, he conceded.

"Probably the storm interfered. Sometime today or tomorrow, someone will come with supplies. They will bring your things from my cabin along with the basket of clothing I packed," she explained calmly. "Until then, I believe that we are expected to spend most of our time in that lovely bed."

"I can't say that would bother me. I peeked out the window and it's *still* raining. Strange how cold it got after that storm, when it was so hot yesterday. A day spent in a warm cozy bed with you sounds perfect," he said softly. "Are you nearly finished eating?"

Her mouth went dry when she saw the intense expression on his face. "I'm finished," she decided abruptly as she shoved her chair back and stood.

"Then come to the fire, baby and get warm," he invited, grabbing her hand and leading her to the spread blanket in front of the warm fire. She saw the brush and comb waiting on the corner of the hearthstone and raised an inquiring eyebrow. "I want to brush your hair," he said, answering her silent query. "Do you mind?"

With silent wonder, she shook her head. Actually, after the oath-binding, wind and rainstorm and the bath before breakfast, it was going to take a while to smooth out all the knots in both of their damp wild manes. Dressing each other's hair seemed like a very intimate thing to do for each other. Considering the extent of their sexual intimacy, Eppie found the idea surprisingly erotic.

He sat with his legs spread and motioned for her to scoot close to him with her back against his chest, between his bent knees. Taking up the brush, he slowly, gently worked the knots from her long hair with revealing patience. It was a sensual, time-consuming process that inexorably built her awareness of Dancer's body as with every gliding stroke through the silky dark strands, he shifted, brushing against her with his chest, arms and legs. The hard length of his cock was a continual presence, rubbing her soft ass. His warm musky male scent surrounded her until she struggled to breathe. At last, he murmured, "Finished. I love your hair."

She moved away from him on shaky limbs and took a deep breath. "My turn." Moving around behind him, she knelt and gathered his hair so that she could rub her hard nipples against the smooth skin of his back. "Hmm. You feel so good. So warm... I didn't know it would be like this," she whispered.

"So do you and it isn't always like this. I think we got very lucky," he said, flexing against her soft curves. "I've never felt this with any other woman."

"Hand me the brush," she directed. When he passed it back to her over his shoulder, she sat back on her heels and began to work the tangles from his hair. As she teased the knots from the soft golden strands, her body inevitably brushed against his hard muscled back. By the time she admitted that her task was complete, both of them were shaking with awareness and need.

He turned to face her, removed the brush from her hands and blindly tossed it into the corner and then pulling her down in his arms, sprawled out on the blanket in front of the fire. With swift, jerky, almost rough movements, he settled her beneath him and positioned his aching cock at the wet entrance of her soft swollen pussy. "I don't think we're going to make it to that bed just yet," he muttered before filling her in one long smooth thrust.

They both stopped to catch their breath. She closed her eyes, savoring the sensation of being filled to capacity. "What ever gave you that idea?" she replied breathlessly.

He slowly withdrew almost all the way, before thrusting so that he could feel the warm wet clasp of her sheath. "Oh, maybe because I can't seem to keep away from you?" He had wanted to take his time, but her body held an irresistible lure. With startling swiftness, their climaxes caught them together in a maelstrom of heat and bright sharp sensation.

# Chapter Thirteen

∞

Over the next two weeks, their time together rushed by in a mass of jumbled impressions for Dancer. Most of their time was spent exploring their overpowering fascination with each other. Eppie, of course, had limited previous experience to compare it to, but Dancer had certainly had enough encounters to know that he had never experienced such seductive need for a woman before. In the few spare moments not taken up with sleeping or eating, he struggled with the ongoing task of assimilating the changes in his surroundings. The simplest things were complicated. It seemed that except for their desire for each other, they had very little in common. She was a gardener and he was an assassin. But then, to be fair, they weren't doing much talking. Perhaps, if they had spent some time away from Stonehollow, it wouldn't have been so very obvious, but in that two weeks, they barely made it out of bed, let alone out of the cottage. One morning, Dancer woke before dawn to the uneasy realization that he wasn't even sure how long he'd been in the valley. Curled around Eppie in their high warm bed, he pondered his actions since arriving in the valley and reluctantly came to the conclusion that he had acted wildly out of character.

Never in his adult life before had he allowed someone else to determine his future. While he didn't feel any powerful urge to repudiate his bonding with Eppie, he resolved that he would have some answers to his questions before the day was over. His determination vibrated so strongly that it woke Eppie from a sound sleep. She didn't know what was bothering him, but clearly something was—enough to wake her. With a silent sigh, she twisted until she could see his face.

"What's wrong?" she asked sleepily.

Warily, he studied her face before replying, "What gave you the idea that something's wrong?"

"Oh, probably because you're sending off such intense waves of decision that it woke me up. Something is bothering you."

Abruptly, he demanded, "How long have I been here? In the valley?"

"I don't know," she admitted, wrinkling her brow in thought. "I can ask Papa or Llyon."

"You don't know either?"

"Well, we've been busy," she pointed out, snuggling closer against his warm body. "I really haven't been paying attention to outside things. Why is this worrying you?"

Tucking her head beneath his chin, he absently rubbed the dark silky strands against his neck. "I don't know," he admitted finally. "It's out of character for me. Under normal conditions I would never lose awareness of my surroundings or circumstances. I don't understand why I've lost myself so completely."

"I'll ask Papa to come talk to us. He will be able to answer your questions." Wriggling around until she could wrap her arms around him, she nuzzled her mouth through the soft golden hair on his chest, seeking a flat copper nipple. When she found it, she suckled lightly, enjoying the sensation of it peaking to a hard point in her mouth.

"What are you doing?"

"Hmm. Nibbling on you?" Shifting, she gradually moved down his body, stopping to kiss and nip his taut muscles along the way. She investigated his navel with her tongue, smiling when she felt his cock growing erect against her breasts. He spread his legs allowing her room to stretch out between them and grasp his aching cock in her warm soft hands. After seriously studying the bounty she held, she slowly, leisurely bathed him with her tongue, earnestly licking every nook and cranny.

"If you're trying to distract me, you're succeeding," he assured her with a soft moan.

"Good. I always like to know I'm pleasing you." With renewed determination, she traced the dark veins with her lips until she reached his plump balls, heavy with the seed that would give her a child. Tenderly, she suckled them in turn before releasing them and returning to the broad tip of his cock to swipe it clean.

He tugged her up his body, huskily demanding, "Ride me, baby. Ride me hard."

She flowed up until she could settle across his hips. Taking his cock in her hands, she rose up enough to position him, sinking down in one long slow movement. Without pause, he slid in to the hilt, feeling her taut internal muscles slowly give way. Immediately, he felt her *schela* grasp him, locking him into place.

When she leaned down to kiss him, he felt the tug of his cock stretching against the lock. She sat back up and announced, "Today, we're going to make a baby. It's time."

Contemplating her pleading expression for several moments as she sat motionless atop him, he finally slowly nodded agreement. "All right. But I think that since I'm providing the necessary seed, you can do the work," he teased. "A joint effort."

"A joint effort." She shifted until she could rub her clit against his hard pubic bone and then proceeded to indeed ride him hard and well. When she finally collapsed on his chest, both of them were exhausted and damp and neither had any doubt that they had succeeded in their mission.

* * * * *

Merlyn and Jade were relaxing in their garden under a tall shady oak tree when a very weary, hot and dusty Dai trotted through the gate. "You made good time," Merlyn observed with a smile as he rose and pulled another chair next to the table. "Come sit down and have something cool to drink."

"I believe I will. Do you realize that the journey from the Hamlet gets longer each time I make it? Twice in two eight-days." He poured a little cool water from the pitcher on his sash and mopped his forehead before winding the sash around his head so that water trickled down through his silver braids. The *chinkas* clinked when he tilted his head in relief. "It's hot on the trail. There's not a breath of breeze even in the shade."

"Was it cooler down at your retreat?" Jade asked softly. "I always loved going there before..."

They all silently contemplated the memories from the time before she lost her sight and then Dai said firmly, "There is no reason for you not to go now, Jade. After Llyon and Tyger have their covenant binding, you and Merlyn should go down to the retreat for a little while. I'll be here to watch over the younglings. And," he pointed out, "you will probably go into *schalzina* or even *schalzah* in the next few weeks."

Merlyn sighed deeply. "So she is pregnant again?"

"As she's known almost since it happened," Dai confirmed sharply. "Haven't you, my Jade?"

"I suppose," she admitted reluctantly. "Just the thought of another baby makes me tired. Do you think this one might be the last one?"

Dai nodded thoughtfully, even though she couldn't see him. "I would say that you're nearing that stage. Already, you're older than any other woman who's borne a child in the valley. I suspect that this one—or two—will be the last."

"Two? Bite your tongue, you old buzzard!" Merlyn slumped back in his chair and closed his eyes. "Two. Don't we have enough without you wishing that on us?"

Dai narrowed his eyes in thought. "It could even be three..."

Jade struggled to her feet and announced with cool dignity, "I have to go take a nap. Dai, I believe we will take you up on your generous offer." Arturo wandered out through the wide doorway leading to the patio and lightly touched his mother's arm. "Ah, Arturo. Just in time to lend me your arm. I need to get some rest. Your papa is going to drag me down to Dai's retreat after your brothers' covenant binding."

"So?" he demanded with a rare smile. "You will enjoy the quiet, you know. And then, when you come back, you'll appreciate the time away even more."

When they had disappeared into the dim coolness of the hallway, Merlyn picked up the second pitcher and poured glasses of mint tea for Dai and himself. "Well? I know you have something on your mind."

"I'm puzzled about the tattoo I observed on Dancer's shoulder at their oath-binding. You are sure it's like mine?"

"Not like it. Identical, Dai. Same colors, same placement, same shape." He leaned back, chugging his tea so that his throat flexed as he swallowed. "It was quite a shock. We knew him when he was just a youngster. He's a genuine music prodigy like Jade. They played a concert together when he was eleven, I think. But he doesn't remember us. Fortunately, he didn't notice our interest in his tattoo because he was so focused on their oath-binding."

"I will go see them," Dai announced with sudden decision. "It's time to check on Eppie and while I'm there, I'll meet her bond mate."

"Do you mind if I come with you?"

"No, of course not. But afterward—when I go out to check on Llyon and Tyger—perhaps you will not come. I think I need to speak to them alone."

Soberly, Merlyn nodded. "That's fine. I wouldn't wish for them to be uncomfortable or embarrassed by my presence. Even though their covenant was expected, I think they'll need time to adjust to having a public relationship." Abruptly, he stood and stretched. "Before we walk out to Stonehollow, I need to check on the rest of the children. Llynx and Panther seem to always find some kind of trouble to get into. Those two have an inexhaustible supply of mischief. Come on into the kitchen when you're ready to go."

"How is Arturo?"

Merlyn froze in the doorway with his back to Dai. "As you saw. Except for the observation tactics class he teaches the younglings, he never leaves the house. Each day he grows more withdrawn."

"He will never get better, beloved, until he faces what happened to him. In some ways, because he is a male, rape is more difficult to recover from than if he was a female, particularly because he is an unpaired *garzhan*. This covenant binding between Tyger and Llyon will magnify his confusion and anger," Dai observed softly.

"I know. What would you have us do?"

"When he's ready, send him down to me at my retreat… That won't be for a while. Until then, I'll keep an eye on him. We wouldn't want a repeat of Tyger's solution."

"God, no!" Merlyn exclaimed before going in to check on his brood.

\* \* \* \* \*

When Dancer wanted to think about something, he cooked. When Eppie worried about something, she cooked. So they spent the afternoon cooking. Baking. Exchanging techniques. It was an eye-opening experience for both of them. It was the first time they spent any length of time together out of bed since their oath-binding.

Dancer introduced her to the concept of a cookbook where she could keep a collection of recipes to share with others. He also demonstrated the use of *measuring utensils*. Eppie, who employed the free-spirited use of the "pinch of this, handful of that" method, laughed out loud at his appalled expression.

"How can you be sure you'll get it exactly the same next time?" he demanded in frustration. "If you don't know how much of each ingredient you used, you can't repeat it. Besides, one of my handfuls is more than one of your handfuls."

"How can you limit yourself to such stringent controls?" she snapped back. "You lose all sense of creativity by sticking to a list on a piece of *linual*!"

Grabbing one of the cookies cooling on the table, he waggled it under her nose. "Here! Try this and tell me it isn't delicious!"

Leaning toward his offering, she bit off a generous hunk and chewed thoughtfully. "Hmm. It is truly delicious, love," she agreed with a twinkle in her eyes.

"But…"

"But, I would have added mint to it," she teased. "And maybe used *quoltania* instead of strawberries. Strawberries are so boring."

Dancer yanked her close enough to cover her smile with his lips. "You are a menace, woman. I can see that I'll have to keep an eye on my utensils," he said, nudging her soft mound with his hard cock.

"Your utensils, huh? Never heard them called that before. But I promise I'll never hurt them." A soft giggle escaped as she leaned back. "Wouldn't want to lose the use of your utensils."

They both froze when an unexpected knock came at the cottage door. "Are we expecting somebody?" he whispered. She shook her head and went to slip on her *meerlim* before shaking out his *sharda* and handing it to him.

"Who is it?" she called out while he fastened the tabs on the *sharda*.

"Dai! And your papa!"

With a shrug and a raised eyebrow, she flashed Dancer a questioning glance before going to open the door. "Hello, Dai! To what do we owe this pleasure?"

Dai quirked an eyebrow and wrinkled his nose. Merlyn merely grinned before commenting, "I hope we weren't interrupting anything."

"Baking," Dancer replied laconically. "Come on in and sample our efforts."

The visitors stood in the doorway and surveyed the laden table and counters with awe. "Who were you planning to feed with this spread?" Dai asked while his mouth watered in anticipation.

"You look like hungry men to me," Dancer replied immediately. "I'll get you some plates and utensils and you can dig in." Eppie watched him bustle around the kitchen, arranging places at the table, setting a savory meat pie between them and pouring them glasses of cool mint tea.

When they were settled and both had full mouths, she tugged Dancer to an empty chair at the table and pushed him down before slipping onto his lap. "Why did you drop by?"

Merlyn shrugged. "It was time to check on you. It's probably too early for you to be pregnant, but then again, maybe not. Anyway, Dai wanted to meet Dancer."

"Uh-huh. Why are you back in Lost Market, Dai?" Eppie asked with a quizzical expression on her face. "I thought you never leave your retreat in the summer."

He swallowed, sipped his tea and then stared at her for a moment. "I've been up here twice since your oath-binding. Once, the next morning to see to Silence because Homer died. And this time to witness Tyger and Llyon's covenant bonding."

"Homer died? What happened? How is Silence? And when did Tyger and Llyon bond?" Eppie demanded.

Yawning mightily, Merlyn sighed. "Everything happened the night of your oath-binding," he answered tiredly. "Ty went into *schalzah* and tried to drown himself. Ly stopped him and offered the covenant. Homer went crazy and tried to kill Silence. They were running around out in the storm when he was struck by lightning. Your mother's pregnant again. Actually, half the younger women in the valley are suddenly pregnant after that storm. Llynx and Panther are grounded again because they broke Marta's window trying to see who could throw a rock the furthest. Cougar pigged out on the blueberry bushes and then threw up all over Wolfe. Falcon accidentally ruined Hawke's small loom so he has to help him make another one. Otherwise, everything is pretty normal."

They all sat in silence, digesting Merlyn's rundown of events. Then cautiously, Dancer observed, "It's a busy man who can deal with attempted suicide, death, broken windows, broken looms, upset stomachs and still find time to get his wife pregnant. I'm surprised you found time to visit us."

"Don't be an ass," Merlyn snapped. "I came with Dai to get away from the chaos for a few minutes. By the way, this meat pie is delicious."

"Save some room for the pizza." Dancer watched the expression on Merlyn's face change to disbelief.

"Pizza? You made pizza?"

"What is pizza?" Dai asked, curious about any food that excited Merlyn.

"It's a flat bread-like crust with tomato sauce and meats and cheeses baked until it's golden brown," Merlyn explained quickly. "What did you use for spices? What about the cheese?"

"I brought spices in my pack. You remember I was escaping...and we're experimenting with the cheese," Dancer replied with a slight smile. "We used that spicy sausage that Eron Burns makes instead of pepperoni."

"When will it be ready?" Merlyn sniffed the air. "Soon, huh?"

"Soon." Dancer nudged Eppie to her feet so he could check the pizza. "What really brought you out here?"

"I wish to see your tattoo," Dai said bluntly.

"Why? It's just a tattoo."

Dai nodded silently. "It is very important to me, though. You will indulge me in this?"

Gently closing the hearth oven door, Dancer shrugged and pulled out a chair next to Dai. Turning it around so he could straddle it, he turned his back to Dai and sat down. If he hadn't been listening so closely, he wouldn't have caught the sharp catch in Dai's throat. Something about his tattoo had upset Dai. "What is it?"

Very softly, Dai said, "Your mother's name was Summer?"

Whipping around to face Dai, Dancer demanded, "Why would you say that?"

Closing his eyes, Dai slumped back in the chair. "So, it's true."

"What do you have to do with my mother, old man?" The question was asked very softly, but beneath the words were a dangerous, roiling snarl.

"Old man, indeed, *grandson*. She was my daughter," Dai revealed calmly. "You are very like her mother, Ilsa. Same hair coloring and eyes."

Time stood still as Dancer stared at Dai, trying to take in the enormity of his news. It wasn't possible. He could not possibly be related to this little gnome of a man, a small blue elfin man with silver hair and wise deep green eyes. Blankly, he looked at Eppie and Merlyn. "You're crazy. From the time I reached this valley, everyone has told me there is no way out. So how could my mother be from here? And why wasn't she blue?"

He got to his feet and paced around the small cottage, muttering curses beneath his breath. "You said that no one could leave. Now the gnome here is trying to convince me he's my grandfather. How the hell could that happen?" Yanking the oven door open, he peeked inside before seizing the folded cloths he was using for potholders. With careful concentration, he slid the pizza onto the wide cutting board that Eppie held for him. Slamming the oven door shut, he turned to Dai. "Well? How did this happen?"

# Chapter Fourteen

ɞ

"I'm not sure," Dai admitted. "I have an idea, but if you're still looking for a way to leave the valley, it won't help you." He studied the young man pacing before the fireplace, noting the tall lean muscular body so very different from his own. Dancer's father must have been very tall, he thought. He wondered what Summer had looked like as an adult. Perhaps she had also been tall—like Ilsa.

Dancer plopped down in the chair next to Dai and softly commanded, "Tell me."

Tilting his head to the side, Dai looked him in the eye and questioned, "You still wish to leave?"

"No." Dancer snorted in derision. "I'm thoroughly bonded to Eppie, just as you all wanted. I simply wish to have the *choice* to leave—even temporarily."

Satisfied, Dai nodded curtly. "I will tell you, but as I said, I'm quite sure you won't find the story of any help." He pointed to Merlyn and Eppie. "They don't know the truth about Ilsa, either, so let us be comfortable for the telling. You will serve this excellent *pizza* and I will share my story."

Accepting Dai's decision with impatient grace, Dancer swiftly cut the pizza and served generous steaming pieces before slipping into the chair next to Eppie. "Done," he announced eagerly.

"Tchk. Such impatience, grandson." Waving his three-tined fork at Dancer, he chided, "The tale won't change anything even if I tell it quickly."

"But, at least you *know*. It's new information for me."

"True. Very true. Well." Dai paused to take another bite and Dancer sighed. "I like this pizza. It's a wondrous dish. Hmmm. When I was young, I bonded with a beautiful woman named Ilsa. In time, we had a lovely little girl born midsummer eve so we named her Summer." Eppie, watching Dai's face with wonder, saw the slow trickle of a tear down his cheek. "When Summer had three years, there was a great forest fire. Here, where Lost Market stands. At that time, it was all woods." He paused and looked off at something only he could see. "Ilsa was an herbalist and she had taken Summer with her on a trip into the woods to search for plants. While they were near here, the fire sprang up and trapped them. Hunters across the river saw Ilsa and Summer on top of Needle Rock. Suddenly, there was a great flash of light and they were gone."

"Needle Rock?" Dancer queried in puzzlement.

"Our judgment stone," Merlyn explained softly. "When we believe someone has committed a crime, we take them to the top of Needle Rock and leave them restrained. If they are guilty, they are consumed by fire. If not, their restraints are destroyed and they come back down."

"If that's so, why do you think Ilsa and Summer survived?"

Dai shrugged. "Normally, there are ashes and bits of bone left. When Ilsa and Summer were taken, there was nothing left. I've been thinking that perhaps the judgment stone sent them somewhere else for safety. There are ancient stories on the Talking Wall about such a thing happening before. Always, it was someone in great danger."

"Mama was found in a church when she was little. The priest thought she was about three or four. A note was pinned to her coat," Dancer said sadly. "It said that her name was Summer and that her mother was dying and could no longer care for her. A childless couple named Smythe adopted her." He sent Dai a peculiar smile. "On her shoulder was the tattoo of a dragon. Her ears had delicate little points near the top and she was always sensitive about them. She never wore her hair pulled back so they showed. You know, it's strange, but since Nanna and Poppy didn't know when her birthday was, they picked July 1st, which is very near midsummer. Three years ago, for her birthday, all of us kids had our left shoulders tattooed with her dragon. She cried for days."

"So, you have siblings? How many?" Dai asked eagerly.

"There were five of us. Now there are two." The cold fury she sensed behind the words chilled Eppie and she shivered. "Two years ago, while Traveller and I were out of the country on an assignment, they were murdered."

After a moment of shocked silence, Dai slowly nodded. "What happened?"

"We don't know exactly," Dancer replied roughly. "We got home that day and stopped by the house first because it was Papa's birthday. Even though it was getting dark, all the lights were out. Trav made some asinine comment about Papa saving on the electricity." He inhaled with a shudder. "We went in the back door like we always do, calling out for Mama and Papa. There wasn't any answer, but we knew right away that something was terribly wrong. We could smell it," he said angrily. "You never forget what death smells like."

"No," Dai agreed sadly.

"Trav tried the lights and they wouldn't come on, so he got the emergency flashlights out of the kitchen junk drawer. Then we went looking."

"You found them?" Merlyn ventured calmly, knowing how very hard it must be to tell the details and yet, with each telling, there would be a tiny, tiny measure of healing.

"Papa was sprawled in the hallway in his pajamas. That told us whatever happened probably was at night because Papa was particular about getting dressed as soon as he woke up. Trav found Teacher in the den. From the damage in there, he put up quite a fight."

"And the others?" Merlyn prodded. Eppie wanted to scream at him to stop, but Dancer merely shuddered and continued.

"It took us a while, but we found Mama in the basement. She had been tortured and took a long time to die, I think. We searched the house, every closet, every possible hiding place—even the attic—but we didn't find Raven or Tracer. Then we called the police."

"They would be suspicious because you searched first."

Merlyn's cool assessment steadied Dancer so that he nodded agreement and finished, "That's the truth. They were really pissed that we had 'messed up' their crime scene, even though we left no prints except the kitchen drawer, light switch and door. One of the cars was missing and they tried to say that Raven and Tracer had done this obscene thing. Then two days later, the car was located in a forest preserve with two bodies in it, burned beyond recognition."

Silence filled the room as each of them absorbed the devastating story. After a while, Dai stirred and stated, "You don't think the bodies were Raven and Tracer. Why?"

"Too convenient," Dancer replied baldly.

"Too neat," Merlyn agreed. "If they didn't know exactly what you and Trav did for a living, they would assume tying up all the loose ends would deflect your questions."

"They were wrong." Shoving back his chair, Dancer rose and started gathering the dishes with barely restrained violence. "At first we were so shocked and furious, we went along with it. Then, when a little time passed, we started picking out the discrepancies. Little things started happening to us. Close calls. Possible accidents that weren't quite accidental. Without knowing who to trust, we started making plans—verbal plans with nothing written down, using the code we made up when we were kids playing spies."

A sudden thought struck Eppie. "What will Traveller do now that you've disappeared?"

Dancer whirled to face her and an unholy smile lit his face. "If he survives—and I certainly expect him to do that easily—he'll follow me. He knows where the cave is. I left him everything he needs. And if anyone gets in his way, they won't stop him for very long. He's much tougher than I am or ever thought about being."

"So. We'll prepare for his arrival," Merlyn said, pursing his lips in thought. "I bet he's really ticked off by the time he gets here. I suppose I better warn whoever's on watch."

"Tell them the code word is *dragon*," Dancer suggested with a wry smile.

"Of course. What else would it be?" With a deep breath, he looked over at Dai and quirked an eyebrow. "Well? Are you ready to leave now? I need to get back home and see what new mischief the children have gotten into and you need to check on Ty and Ly."

Dai nodded briefly. "Yes, I'm ready." He got up from the table and carried his plate and utensils to the sink. "We will leave you alone for now. Eppie, you know, of course."

"About the baby we made? Of course. We both knew immediately." She leaned against Merlyn and kissed his forehead. "Grandpa," she whispered.

He groaned and kissed her back, hugging her tightly. "Babies. Someday you'll all be grown and I won't have to change diapers."

"You're the one that told me it was my job to get her pregnant," Dancer pointed out. "I did my job. I would think that would make you happy."

"You have no idea how happy it makes me. I just didn't plan to have one of my own at the same time!"

"See, that's where pants would be better than a *sharda*," Dancer said with a straight face. "It's so much easier to stay out of trouble if you keep it in your pants than it is in a *sharda*."

"But now that the damage is done, a *sharda* is much more convenient!" With that last retort, Merlyn and Dai went out the door, leaving Eppie and Dancer with a great pile of dirty dishes and pots to keep them occupied the rest of the afternoon.

When Dai reached the Lake House, he found Llyon and Tyger lounging lazily on a blanket on the beach by the lake. The remains of a light meal were piled in a small basket next to them. Even in the heat of the day, Tyger was sprawled face down with his head in Llyon's lap and wrapped in a bathing sheet. Llyon was sitting cross-legged, just dressed in a light *sharda*. He was brushing Ty's hair. From their damp appearance and wet hair, Dai deduced they'd been swimming in the lake and he shuddered. As long as he had been alive, the icy water in the lake had never been warm enough for swimming.

Wordlessly, Dai perched on one of the nearby sections of log that had been purposely cut and set on the beach for rough seating. "So. I have come," he announced unnecessarily. "You are ready for the formal bonding?"

Ty turned his head so he could see Dai's face and asked, "Why does everyone keep asking us if we're sure? Even though Papa and Mama knew this was coming, knew it was inevitable, they asked us over and over if we are sure."

"When were they here?" Dai asked with a faint smile.

"Mama had this notion that we wouldn't survive out here without extra blankets and food, so Papa plopped her in the cart with all the junk they decided we needed and he pushed her out here three days after the storm. You wouldn't believe the stuff they brought," Llyon said with a quirk of his brow. "It took us two days to find a place to put all of it."

"They're still getting over just how close they came to losing both of you," Dai chided gently. "It's no small thing to lose one child, let alone two. They're scared and shocked and don't want you to think it's because of your bonding."

Ty sat up and wrapped the bathing sheet closer around his chest. "You're saying that our bonding didn't bother them?"

Dai shook his head. "Of course not. They've expected it for nearly twenty years. In the past few years, they expected it daily — to the point that some of your family was ready to bang your heads together so you would get on with it. Your entire family, all of your friends and most of your neighbors are breathing a sigh of relief."

"Then I repeat. Why does everyone keeping asking us if we're sure?"

"Perhaps because they can't believe that you finally woke up and realized you belonged together?" Dai stared at him quizzically. "You were very stubborn and very slow. Even Cougar and Gazelle were beginning to make plans of ways to get you together."

"Oh? What did they have in mind?" Llyon asked as he concentrated on braiding Tyger's hair.

Dai laughed. "It would have worked. They were going to trick you into going in the tiny guest hut out near Eppie's cabin and then lock you in. I think they had some scheme to also get your clothes away from you."

"That might have worked," Ty agreed with a mighty yawn. "I was getting desperate and so was Llyon. We just couldn't seem to find the courage to talk about it. What we had was better than nothing."

"And what you have now was worth the loss of your loom?"

Tyger flinched. "Yes. Even the loss of my loom is worth being with Llyon," he replied steadily. "The loom can be replaced. Being with him can't."

"Well, then. I have come to oversee your bonding. Tomorrow at noon, eh?"

"Sure." Llyon fastened off the last braid and tapped Ty on the shoulder. "My turn."

While Tyger stood, dressed and moved to sit behind Llyon, Dai inquired, "Who do you wish to stand for you?"

"Mama and Papa," Llyon replied softly. "We were going to ask Arano and Arturo but Ty said that Arturo would find it painful and after I thought about it, I have to agree." He tilted his head so that Tyger could work the broad-toothed comb through a tough tangle. "I don't know what to do for him, Dai. He's hurting and I can't help him."

"I've spoken to your papa about it. When he's ready, he'll come down to the retreat and I will deal with him. Until he faces what happened to him, he won't get any better." Abruptly, Dai smiled and changed the subject. "There is much going on in the valley. Your mama is pregnant again. Eppie is pregnant. Actually, as of this morning, I know of twenty-three women who are pregnant."

Llyon turned his head, wincing when Ty inadvertently caught the comb in another knot and stared at Dai in astonishment. "What's going on?"

"Dancer and Eppie's bonding storm, I think." He shrugged. "I can't think of what else it might be. So, be ready to deal with that when you come back. Your mama said to tell you that you're going to be living in Eppie's cabin. By the time she and Dancer finish their time at Stonehollow your old compartment will be ready for them. And there is certainly room for another baby in the nursery."

"And how are they doing?" Ty asked absently as he began to braid Llyon's hair. "Still panting after each other like a couple of *dintis*?"

"More so," Dai acknowledged dryly. "I just came from there. The cottage smelled like nonstop sex, lightly coated with the odor of cooking, since they'd been baking this morning. I suspect that they were naked when we got there and had to dress before they could open the door."

Tyger grinned at Dai. "Probably. Is he still looking for a way out of the valley?"

"Not so much," Dai said, studying Ty's braiding critically. "He's my grandson so he's not as anxious to leave now."

The twins froze for a moment, then both turned to stare at Dai in accusation. "What?" they demanded in unison.

With deceptive calm, Dai related all that he knew, suspected and everything that Dancer had shared with him. When he was finished, both Tyger and Llyon stared at him with disbelief. Finally, Llyon said, "That's quite a tale, Dai. How did Dancer take it?"

"He was upset." Dai's pithy understatement drew a smile from both the younger men.

Tyger nodded thoughtfully. "I suspect that he must be finding the daily adjustments very difficult. It must seem as though he's being bombarded with changes and new information at every turn."

"From what you've told us, Dai, it has been a terrible time for him for quite a while. I would be very angry if such a thing had happened to Mama and Papa and the younglings," Llyon said soberly. "Such anger and grief would not be put away lightly. Nor would it be easy to walk away, knowing that he can never go back and therefore, will never know what really happened—especially to Tracer and Raven. There will never be justice for their deaths. It would take a powerful incentive to leave that behind."

"It was," Dai agreed dryly. "Someone was trying to kill him. And Traveller. While I was walking here, it occurred to me that part of the reason he is so anxious to leave the valley is because he's worried about Trav. Even though he believes that Traveller is capable of defending himself, apparently there were several incidents that were made to appear as accidents that were not. Both of them are sure they were clever attempts to get rid of them. If that is so, then the reason for his anxiety and restlessness is obvious."

"It also explains why he was so angry when Eppie bit him at their oath-binding. Clearly, he wasn't so angry about the bite as he was at what he saw as a betrayal. If he's spent three years watching his back every second, I can see why he was upset." Tyger finished the last braid and slipped his arms around Llyon's shoulders, hugging him with fierce emotion. "I'm so glad that Ly and I have each other. It was lonely until that night here at the lake. I can't imagine having to walk away from him now."

"Well," Dai sighed before he stood and brushed his *sharda*, "I should be going back to your parents' dome. I have invited them to go down to my retreat for a while and I volunteered to watch over the younglings while they are gone."

"You're insane," Tyger pointed out. "You must be to volunteer to watch Panther and Llynx. They'll give you more gray hair than you already have."

"Wrinkles, too, no doubt," Dai agreed. "However, your parents are finding the thought of another unexpected baby — or two — a little stressful. I believe your Mama had her mind set that Cougar and Gazelle were the last ones."

Llyon gathered up the blanket, shook it firmly and began to fold it. "I think perhaps this pregnancy will be the last. I know she looks much younger than she is, but she's already older than any other woman in the valley who's carried a baby."

"I have told her as much, just this afternoon. She is healthy and active, but we will have a care with her anyway. She'll probably be a terrible patient." Dai sighed again. "Enough. I must go. I will see you in the bonding circle beyond Silence's dome tomorrow at noon." Without another word, he strode off across the meadow, picking his way around the soggy areas that were still drying out from the storm and flood.

# Chapter Fifteen

**ೋ**

Paullie woke knowing that he was just seconds from death. The knife piercing the skin just below his right ear pressed a smidgeon deeper and he felt the warm trickle of blood run down his neck to his pillow. "Dancer?" he whispered carefully.

"Try again," a deep gravelly voice suggested and he nearly had heart failure.

"Traveller?" he whimpered and felt the bed under him grow warm when he lost control of his bladder. If Dancer was a bad dream when crossed, his brother Traveller was an unremitting nightmare.

"Very good," that dark voice purred. "Now let's see if we can come to terms, Paullie. You tell me where Dancer is and I'll decide how long it's going to take you to die." As Traveller perched on the boxy night stand next to his head, his long thick braid flicked the side of Paullie's face. "I think you should begin now," he prodded gently.

Paullie moaned. "I don't know where he is. Please…"

"But you know something about it, Paullie. When you woke up, you assumed right away that I was Dancer, so…" he trailed off suggestively.

Swallowing carefully, Paullie licked lips suddenly gone very dry. "The Old Man sent us after this target. Halfway up the mountain, we got caught in a blizzard and we barely got back down alive. But when we left Bright Shadows Mountain, Dancer was still alive. He kept just out of reach…"

"And this was when?" Trav queried, delicately twisting the knife.

Paullie whimpered again. "Ahhh, don't please. It was four weeks ago! Saturday!"

Trav sighed quietly. "Now suppose you tell me exactly why Free decided to wipe him?"

"We heard Dancer quit...wanted to retire. The Old Man didn't like that." In a burst of confidence, he added, "He was packing some kind of big case or bag when we saw him, like he planned to stay awhile."

"Paullie, Paullie, what am I going to do with you?" The dark velvet tones had a contemplative quality. Paullie held very still, trying to appear as small as an insignificant mouse.

"I never saw you. I never heard of you. I'll leave for Mexico in the morning!" Paullie offered desperately.

"Do you know what? I think I want you to give Free a message for me, Paullie. Do you think you could do that for me?" he asked gently, but with razors in his voice.

"Sure, sure, I can do that," Paullie assured him frantically. "I can absolutely give him any message you want!"

"In the morning—on your way to Mexico—I would like you to call Free. And you might mention that I'm a trifle annoyed with him, Paullie. As a matter of fact, I'm so annoyed that I've decided to tender my resignation," he decided thoughtfully. "And since he's seen fit to make my only brother disappear, I think that I'll take Bish, just as a trade, you know? Don't you think Bish would be a fair trade?" he queried gently. "After all, he's the only one of the Llewellyns get that has any honor."

"Oh, God," Paullie moaned. "He's going to kill me. He's going to *kill* me!"

"Now, Paullie, you're going to Mexico, remember?" He shifted minutely and another slow trickle of blood fell to the pillow. "Hmm. You might also mention that I would be *delighted* to entertain any of his tame little Boy Scouts who he wants to send to visit. I'm sure that we could find something for them to do..."

Quivering with dread, Paullie kept his mouth shut. He felt the tiny prick of the needle and slid into sleep before Traveller folded his pocket knife and slipped it back into his pocket.

It had been a busy week for Trav. After emptying Dancer's safe and escaping to Chuin's attic, he had plenty of time to plan. There was absolutely nothing he cared about except his brother. There was absolutely nothing he would not do to find him. There was absolutely no one he wouldn't kill to protect him. Using every skill and contact that he dared, Trav prepared to follow him. When he was ready, he just needed one last thing—a hostage to keep Free off his back.

He knew exactly where to get everything he required in one place. His good buddy, Bishop Llewellyn would be the perfect hostage and he just happened to own the perfect vehicle. In his secret basement the other requirements for the plan were concealed behind a hidden door. Yeah, Bishop would be perfect.

Bish Llewellyn woke with the certainty that it was *not* going to be a good day. His head was full of tiny elves industriously beating on drums. His stomach was jumping in time to the drum beating. And his arms were twisted uncomfortably behind his back, where they appeared to be tied to his ankles. No, it wasn't going to be a good day. A dark bag that seemed to be impregnated with cow manure was pulled over his head. He sincerely hoped that most of the cow manure had been emptied from the bag before he had dubious pleasure of its acquaintance. As he carefully took stock of his situation, he realized that he was stark naked and cold and had been rather carelessly dumped on the rough metal floor of a moving vehicle. It was a stupid way to spend his forty-fifth birthday.

The speed at which the vehicle seemed to be moving down a dry river bed did not auger well for either the vehicle or his skin. He bounced from one side to the other and concluded with faint resignation that he had no hope of getting out of this situation with a whole skin. The vehicle slammed to a stop and he heard the driver get out and shut the door. A few seconds later, the back door was opened and he was yanked toward the opening, losing more skin on the way. Almost with relief, he felt the tiny needle prick in his ankle and then he knew no more.

When he woke next, the elves were still with him, he was stretched out on the ground with his arms and legs firmly tied to stakes and he was still naked. The bag had been removed from his head and he saw that he was surrounded by darkness. About six feet away, a small fire was merrily crackling, but it provided no heat for him. The duct tape that had covered his mouth had obviously been ripped off, taking part of his skin and mustache with it. It still burned, so he decided he was glad that he had not been conscious for that particular delight. His field of vision was limited, but it seemed to him that he was in a cave.

"Well, well. I see you decided to finally rejoin the almost living," a dark velvety voice observed and he knew exactly why he was in this situation.

"'Lo, Trav," he said casually. "Lots of work to piss off my father."

"Now, Bish," he was assured, "nothing is too much work to piss off your father." Traveller moved into his field of vision and looked down at him. "You don't look very comfortable, Bish. Aren't you cold, like that?"

"Freezing," Bish replied curtly. "But I'm sure you have something in mind to warm me up, so I'm not too worried about it." He shivered artistically, but Trav wasn't buying. "So, what's the deal? Are we waiting for a party? Or is this a stag deal?"

"Just you and me," Trav informed him agreeably. "Straight trade. You for Dance."

"And if Dad doesn't have Dancer?" Bish devoutly hoped that his father had Dancer.

"We-ll, we'll get to be really close friends." Traveller laughed quietly, sending chills up Bishop's back. "I *do* hope that your father believes that I won't negotiate." He moved away and Bish heard the sound of liquid splashing into a container. "Are you thirsty?"

"I could use some water," Bish replied.

"Here. Turn your head," Trav instructed as he held a metal cup to Bish's mouth. "There are approximately six hundred men out there on the mountain, trying to pinpoint this position," he said casually, as he tossed his heavy auburn braid back over his shoulder. "If they get too close, the entire canyon this cave opens onto is going to become a solid wall."

"Dynamite?"

"Something better." He stood and walked away with the cup. "I gave your father detailed instructions, which he seems to be having difficulty following. But then, I always thought that Harry was probably really running the show…"

"And after you blow the canyon?" Bish asked, praying that Trav had an escape route planned.

"Oh, we'll wait in complete comfort for the air to run out," Trav answered calmly. "If you want, I'll even untie you. Sorry, I don't have any clothes for you, but it was a come as you are party and that's how you were. I can give you a blanket."

"What if Dad can't produce your brother?"

"Well, I'll be really sorry about that, but he should have let Dancer retire. Your father knew the job was tearing Dance apart after those kids died." Trav drank from the cup, before tossing the dregs to the side. "Dancer wasn't ever the same."

There didn't seem to be anything useful to say, so Bish kept his mouth shut. He hoped his father was considering all the options. Of all the things that Traveller could have pulled, taking one of the sons of Free Llewellyn was the one most likely to get his attention. After his son, Baron and his daughter-in-law, Jade, had been abducted, they were never seen again. Free had never quite gotten over that, even after more than twenty-five years. He sighed.

"I don't suppose you would like to let me go to the bathroom…"

"I might be able to arrange it," Trav conceded. He moved away for a moment and returned with a bundle of sturdy plastic strips that Bish recognized. Used in differing combinations, they could serve as temporary restraints for almost any situation. He put together an efficient hobble and attached it to his ankles. Leaving one ankle staked, he moved up to work on his wrists. When they were secured, he pulled up the remaining stakes and hoisted Bish to his feet. Pointing him in the direction of the far corner, he waited for him to shuffle off.

"What, no hands?" Bish complained.

"Improvise. If it's going to be too difficult, I'll start thinking that you really don't need to go."

Bish shuffled off to the corner, taking his time. When he reached the corner, he leaned his head against the wall and aimed with mixed results. He heard the sound of a rifle shot and then the cave seemed to jump up and shake him like a dog.

When the vibrations rippled away, he saw Traveller stretched out in the dirt across the cave from him. Incredibly, the fire still burned, though it looked as though the tidy little pile of wood was somewhat scattered. In the distance, he could hear a low rumbling and somewhere, deep inside, he knew that they were trapped. Lucky shot. Or unlucky shot, if you were the fella that was going to answer to his father. Shaking his head, he shuffled over to Trav's body, hoping that he wasn't dead yet. He didn't particularly want to be shut up in a cave with a body for company.

"Trav?" He could see his chest moving, so that meant he was still breathing. "Trav! Wake up!"

"Why?" he answered quietly.

"Because I would like to be untied now. That was the deal. The canyon goes down, I get to be untied," Bish reminded him reasonably.

"I seem to recall that the deal was based on *me* blowing the stuff, not some idiot with a rifle for a brain." He sighed. "I've always said that they let any fool jackass carry a gun. Too bad, they don't know what to do with them. Well, don't stand there. Get over here and dig my knife out of my pocket."

Bish studied him thoughtfully. Trav wasn't moving and that was a very bad sign. "How badly are you injured?"

"Well, I think that pretty well every thing that can break is broken," Trav replied calmly. "I seem to be breathing, so I'm not sure about my neck or spinal cord...and I seem to be feeling plenty of pain, so I suppose that's a good sign—if I was within a reasonable distance to a hospital. Even my hair hurts."

"Want me to cut it off?" Bish offered, squatting down next to him. "Which pocket is the knife in?"

"The right one. And if you cut my hair, there won't be a place on Earth I won't find you."

Moving like a lame duck, Bish carefully turned around with his back to Trav. "You're going to have to tell me when I get in the general vicinity. I don't want to touch you any more than I have to until these manacles are off."

"That's handsome of you after all of this," Trav observed.

"Well, you're right about Dance. Dad should have let him go." He moved down a couple of inches. "How far now?"

"Back toward my head, just about an inch." Trav was in so much pain, his vision was blurring. He felt Bish catch the edge of his pocket and then when he slid his fingers inside, Trav passed out.

"Trav?" When no response was forthcoming, Bish privately thought that the faint might be for the best. Fishing out the knife, he worked it open and sliced through the plastic ties. When Bish finally had them off, he found a couple of nicks, but overall, he was satisfied that he hadn't sliced a finger off. A couple of slices later, his ankles were free and he stood up. He located Trav's flashlight and wormed his way up the passage to the canyon far enough to confirm that they were definitely trapped. With a deep sigh, he twisted around and returned to the cave.

Prowling around, he checked through Trav's piles of junk, happy to locate a blanket and a sleeping bag. He found the water and had another long drink. He built the fire up and then checked Trav's pulse and found it surprisingly strong. Methodically, starting at the top, he checked for breaks, bleeding and internal injuries. After a quick inventory check, he decided that there wasn't much he could do for him, except slide him into his sleeping bag, while he was still unconscious. There were no breaks with obviously displaced bones and without Trav's input, he wasn't going to mess with him. If they *did* get out of this mess somehow, he didn't want Trav paralyzed because of something he did. He rummaged through the boxes and things piled against the back wall, looking for something he could use for a backboard, finally settling for a large box, which he had to empty.

He was quite pleased to find some high-energy food bars and a bag of apples. These he set aside, while he continued to dump things on the floor. Near the bottom, he found a pair of nylon pull-on jogging shorts and a ratty t-shirt and that made his day complete. He stood up, slipped them on and felt much better at once. Whatever the religious folks might say, he didn't want to meet his maker in the altogether.

When he had the box empty, he broke it down, flattened and folded until he felt he had a manageable size to work with. He duct taped every seam and fold first, then proceeded to wrap the entire piece in duct tape for extra strength. When that was finished, he set it aside and had an energy bar and cup of water. Then he looked for something he could use to brace

Trav's neck. After a while, he found a towel, so he set that with his back board.

"Been busy?" Trav's slurred words shook him out of his reverie.

"Very. Glad to see you're back." Bishop brought him a cup of water and a spoon. He carefully spooned small sips into his mouth. "How's it going?"

"I'm not a very happy camper right now," Trav admitted. "I've decided that I'm going to track down the happy hunter and beat the crap out of him, just as soon as I can."

Bish smiled in spite of himself. "Sounds like a plan to me. Is anything hurting so bad it stands out?"

"No. There's just one big ocean of pain." Trav looked up at the ceiling. "Bish, check the ceiling. That piece looks like it's loose."

Bishop found a flashlight and checked over the entire ceiling. He found two spots that didn't look very good. "Well, I've got bad news and bad news. Which do you want first?"

"Oh, I think I'll settle for the bad news."

"We've got two spots that don't look so hot. If I drag you to the very back, we should be safe if it comes down."

"Okay, what's the bad news?"

"If the ceiling comes down, we'll have about a six by six space back there."

"Cozy. I told you we were going to be real good friends." Trav smiled grimly. "Good thing you found those clothes, or we might have gotten to be better friends than we wanted, huh?"

"What a scary thought." He retrieved his backboard, sleeping bag, towel and duct tape. "Listen, before this ceiling does come down, I want to get you settled." He explained what he thought he could do and Trav agreed, though as he pointed out, there wasn't much he could do about it if he *didn't* agree. "Once I have you taped into this contraption, I'm going to move you back there in that corner."

"Okay. Better move the water and food back there, too. And Dancer's violin and guitar," he insisted stubbornly.

"All right, all right. I'll find his violin and guitar, though why in the world you want them, I wouldn't know. For damned sure, you can't play them." Bish went to locate them and carry them to the back wall. When he had everything settled he came back to Traveller. "Okay, everything's set. Are you ready?"

"As ready as I will ever be," Trav mumbled. "Bish, if I flake out, or drop dead, don't worry. You did your best, you know?"

"You will not die. I refuse to let you, because then Dancer would hunt me down and one of you is enough to deal with," Bish declared.

It was not anything that Bish ever wanted to do again, but eventually, he had Trav arranged on the back board, with the neck brace, in the sleeping bag. The last job was dragging him to the back of the cave. After taking a short break, it occurred to him that it would be a good notion to pile everything else in a barricade across their space. If the ceiling came down, perhaps the barricade would hold the ceiling up enough that they would have a breathing space. He was determined that he was going to give them every chance for a successful rescue.

When he had his barricade constructed, he wrapped himself in the blanket and lay down next to Trav. He planned to stay awake, but it had been a busy day, what with abductions and explosions and soon he was fast asleep.

Bish wasn't certain of what woke him, but abruptly, he was wide awake. He saw that Trav's eyes were open. "What is it?"

"I don't know, but something's not right. I woke up a couple of minutes ago and I've been lying here, trying to figure out what's bothering me." His eyes flickered around their space. "I smell roses."

"Roses? In December?"

"And the air is warmer back here. I can feel a drift of warm air on my face. See if you can locate the source."

Bishop unwrapped his blanket and found the flashlight. "If there's a way out, we can get you some help…" he began.

"Bish. I'm not worried about getting out of here. If Dance is gone, there isn't much left for me." He sighed quietly. "I shouldn't have dragged you into it. I think I went a little crazy for a while. Take the violin and guitar in case Dancer shows up, okay?"

His friend frowned down at him. "Tell you what. The instruments only go if you go. So if you want Dancer to have them, you better give them to him yourself. Now, I'm going to find our phantom roses."

It took him thirty minutes to locate the opening. It was such a clever optical illusion, that eventually he only found it by running his hands along the wall. He investigated the first twenty feet and returned. "We can get out this way, Trav. It will be tight in some places, but I can drag you behind me." Faint rumbles near the front of the cave made their decision for them. Bish had found some rope in one of the boxes. He laced and knotted together the things they were taking with them so that he could drag them behind him. Then inch by inch, he wormed through the passage. It was time-consuming, exhausting work. Move a little. Drag Trav. Drag the stuff. Move forward a little more. By his reckoning, a little over two hours later, they reached the other end.

With a sigh of relief, he pulled the last of the things into the new cavern. After a careful reconnoiter, he was satisfied that they were safe for the night. He found a fairly level space and dragged Trav there. Trav had long since fainted, so after checking his pulse, Bishop let him sleep. He piled the rest of their belongings around them, wrapped his blanket around him and stretched out next to Trav to sleep.

# Chapter Sixteen

**ß)**

Another week in the valley had soothed much of Dancer's anxiety. He meditated on all that Dai had told him of his mother's history and because the pieces fit together so completely, he reluctantly concluded that Dai's version of events was probably the truth. When he remembered how anguished his Mama was because of the mystery behind her abandonment, he wished she could have known that Dai had never forgotten her. Ilsa must have been very close to death to have abandoned her daughter so completely. He mourned for all of them and what might have been.

Eppie watched him struggle with the newest blows and did her best to comfort him as he came to terms with his ever-changing life. The sharing of his story seemed to open the dam and with increasing frequency, he talked about his life before his arrival in the valley. At first, he mostly mentioned things he had done with Trav, good memories that made him smile.

Then by the end of the week, under her gentle ministrations, he started talking about his parents and other siblings. His pain was a living, breathing presence with them once the barriers were down, but Eppie sensed the slow healing that was taking place each time he talked about his missing loved ones.

One day, he pulled his pack—which Wolfe had finally delivered—from beneath the bed and emptied it out on the table, slowly sorting the contents into small piles as he went. Eppie watched, fascinated at the strange variety of items strewn in front of her. He pulled the gardening book from the pack, dug out the seed packets and plopped them down under her nose. She crooned in delight as she sorted and studied the information on the packets before turning to the book. Her amazement at the pictures and drawings was profound. When he showed her the index and explained how she could find any subject she wanted, her eyes widened, then sparkled with joy. It's possible that she would have sat there poring over the pictures for another week, but the growing mound of strange articles pulled her attention away from the gardening book, though she kept one hand firmly planted on top.

Of all the things he pulled out, she found his briefs the most amusing. From the time he entered the valley until their oath-binding, he had only worn boxers—or nothing at all. She held the white stretchy cotton briefs up, turning them over in her hands, investigating the placket in the front and shot him a questioning glance. "What are these?"

"Underwear. Shorts. Briefs. Tighty-whities. They're called a lot of things," he replied absently as he continued to rummage in his bag.

"Clothing?" She turned them over again, puzzled at their purpose. "How do you wear them?"

"Under your pants," he explained, before asking quizzically, "Do you want me to model them?"

"Model?"

"Put them on and demonstrate," he elaborated patiently. He took the pair of briefs from her, stood back from the table and slipped them on.

She leaned forward and fingered the placket. "And this? What is this for?"

Bending over until his nose touched hers, he whispered, "*Availability*." At her startled look, he fished his cock out through the opening, demonstrating its use.

Immediately, she wanted to try this new game for herself. After slipping his cock in and out of the briefs several times, it was iron-hard, dark red and he was groaning. She licked her lips, then took him in her warm, wet mouth and sucked enthusiastically, flickering around the sensitive head with her tongue.

"Eppie, I'm not going to last long at this rate," he warned. She redoubled her efforts and moments later he came with a shout that echoed around the cottage. After she meticulously licked him clean, she gently tucked him back inside the briefs with a soft pat on the placket.

"I like your underwear," she observed with a small merry grin. "You must wear them often for me."

He sprawled bonelessly down in a chair and nodded agreement. "Anytime, baby. Anytime."

"What is this other stuff?"

With a sigh, he sat up and went back to his sorting. "This is a computer. I'll show you later how it works. It won't work for long because you don't have electricity here to recharge the batteries." Pawing through a few more things, he set them in front of her. "Here are a couple of books. *Pilgrim's Progress.* The Bible. Here is a first-aid kit. Your Papa or Llyon might like that…" He set several small plastic bottles of spices in front of her. "Put these in the cabinet, they're spices and herbs for cooking."

She picked one up, studying the label with interest. "What is *paprika?*"

"A spice. I'll show you how to use it next time we cook," he promised as he set another thick book in front of her. It was bound with a wire spiral along one side, had a picture of a delicious looking plate of food on the cover and the words across the top, *Kitchen Kompositions* picked out in dark green letters, shaded with gold. Near the bottom of the cover in smaller print it read, *by Dancer Devereaux.*

She tenderly rubbed the letters with one finger as she read them in astonished realization. "You wrote a book! It has your name on it!"

"It's a cook book," he pointed out wryly, "not the Great American Novel. It has recipes that use *measurements*, so I don't know if you'll want to use it."

She ignored his teasing as she flipped through the pages, stopping occasionally when something caught her interest. "This is wonderful, Dancer. How exciting it must have been to see your name in print!"

He wondered what she would have thought if she knew the truth about his life out-valley and just how frequently his name and picture were both published. He had a notion that she would very quickly get over the awe of having his name in print.

Abruptly, she stood and carried the books to the mantel, where she cleared a spot for them and reverently set them in place. Returning to the table, she gathered up the spice bottles and carried them over to the cabinet and put them away. The seed packets she placed on the counter, eager to plant them in some starter containers and watch them grow. "What else?"

"My bamboo flute, my small pan pipes, a harmonica..." he said, placing them all together. "Here's some CDs and a CD player. We'll listen later this evening. Once the batteries run out, it won't be any good, either."

"CDs?"

"Music. I'll show you later." He folded his clothing hastily and stuffed it back in the bag. "If I'd known I wasn't going to be wearing clothes, I would have left some of this stuff behind and filled the bag with other stuff," he muttered. "Hmmm. Here's another book. Tracer wrote this one, it's about ancient and antique musical instruments. You might find it interesting." He placed it on the table near her and went back to his sorting. "Tea packets. Pain meds. Shaving kit—no need for that now. Crochet hooks. Needle and thread. Tool kit. Blank sheet music. Notebook and pens... I should keep a journal, I suppose." Muttering beneath his breath, he continued to move things around. "Weapons, ammo, gloves…" he murmured, piling them on his right. "A space blanket, pictures and personal papers, Swiss army knife, duct tape and a cross-stitched cloth my mother made. I bet Dai would like to see that."

"May I?" she asked, reaching for it.

"Sure."

She caught her breath when she unfolded it and saw the dragon intertwined with a snarling lion. Below it were glyphs that read, "Perseverance, Passion and Loyalty."

"What is it?" he asked, curious at her reaction.

"The glyphs. They're the Janusai family motto."

"Janusai?"

"Dai's last name is Janusai," she explained gently. "The dragon is his family symbol. The lion is mine. Your mother embroidered our family symbols intertwined."

Cold sweat broke out on his back and neck. He took the needlework from her and carefully refolded it before replacing it in his pack. "How could my mother possibly know these things?"

Before she could answer, a rapid tattoo was tapped out on their door. Once again, they rapidly dressed and Eppie went to the door. Wolfe strode agitatedly to and fro on the porch, waiting impatiently for them to answer.

"What's wrong?" Dancer demanded immediately when he saw Wolfe's face.

"More strangers in the valley," Wolfe gasped out. "Papa has gone to see. Dai is there and says one man is badly injured. Be wary. When Papa knows more, he will tell us."

"Traveller?"

Wolfe shook his head. "I don't know. I will come back when I know more."

Dancer closed the door, for the first time securing it with the bar, before returning to the pile of weaponry on the table. Methodically, he cleaned and prepared everything before placing it in readiness on the small stand next to the door. If trouble came, he would be ready.


When Bish woke, a very old, smallish blue man was leaning over Traveller. He had both hands spread out over him and was slowly moving them along Trav's body as though he could see through the skin with them. The man noticed that he was awake and nodded to him. "Your friend is badly hurt," he announced. "I've called for help to move him."

"Who are you?" Bish asked in puzzlement. He had never seen anything like this guy. He had very long silver hair, arranged in a multitude of small braids, each finished with a jeweled clasp. When he moved, it sounded like a delicate wind chime. His face reminded Bish of a withered apple, except for those bright, twinkling green eyes. He thought they were bird eyes. He had some sort of cloth wrapped around his lower body and soft leather sandals.

"I am Dai."

"Uh-huh. And who are you when you're home, Die?" Bish's brows rose in query.

"I am Dai. A healer." He looked directly at Bishop. "Your friend is in need of a healer." His head came up as he heard people approaching. "Good. Help has arrived and soon your friend will be more comfortable."

Shoving the blanket away, Bish got to his feet. No one was going to move Trav until he talked to somebody that made more sense. Several people appeared on the pathway behind the waterfall shielding the cave, all talking at once. When they saw Bish, the babble stopped abruptly as though cut with a knife.

The oldest man in the group tilted his head to one side, smiled widely and said calmly, "Hello, Bishop. Fancy meeting you here."

Bish knew that voice though he hadn't heard it in years. He sat down so suddenly he had bruises on his backside for a week. He shook his head very slowly and then just stared. "Baron." His eyes grew round with shock as he really looked at him. Baron's black hair, shot through with silver streaks now, was arranged like the old man's hair. He wore the same soft skirt-like garment with matching vest and the soft sandals. And his skin was *blue*. Almost absently, he noted the gently pointed ears and the flash of fangs when Baron smiled. After a minute, he realized that he was opening and closing his mouth like a goldfish, but no sound was coming out. He tried again but it came out as a hoarse croak. "Baron."

Merlyn came and squatted down next to him, with his arm across his shoulder. "Bish, I'm glad to see you." He gestured for the others to come closer. "This is part of my family. Llyon. Tyger. Wrenna. And two men from our village, Jonas and Mali. And you remember Jade, don't you?" Yes, he remembered Jade, but she looked quite different with her glowing auburn hair bound up in some kind of braided coronet arrangement sprinkled with tiny jewels. He had never seen her when her hair was this neat. They were all blue…

After looking at the strange group, Bish turned to his brother, "Baron, why have you never let us know that you were okay?"

Merlyn stood and helped his brother to his feet. "That's a long story, Bish and we'll have plenty of time to tell it. Why don't we get this man settled and then we can talk." He looked down at Trav with a puzzled frown. "This man looks like Dancer."

"How do you know Dancer?" Bish was finding the entire encounter stranger by the second.

Llyon and Dai worked with quiet haste to stabilize Traveller while Wrenna knelt near his head. Suddenly she slumped over with her head resting on his shoulder. Tyger jumped to pull her away but Dai shook his head. "Leave her, Ty. They're in *rapport* and it's better if they're touching."

More confused than ever, Bishop turned to his brother and demanded, "What's going on? What is she doing?"

Merlyn took his arm, turning him away from the group working on Trav. "Wrenna is his mate. She's helping them stabilize him by linking with him mind to mind. You needn't worry about him. We certainly wouldn't want to have to face Dancer if something happened to Traveller!"

"You didn't answer me before. How do you know Dancer?"

A small smile crept across his face as Merlyn replied proudly, "He's my bond-son." Observing the panicked look on Bish's face, he suggested kindly, "Look! You're very tired and your friend needs immediate attention. Come with us and I assure you that we will explain everything as soon as possible."

Wrenna, with the help of Tyger, got to her feet and joined her father and Bishop. Taking him by the hand she suggested, "Why don't you come with Mama and me, Uncle Bishop? Traveller is your friend."

Unsure of how it had happened, he found himself outside the cave, moving across a tiny clearing toward a lushly blooming valley, with Jade and Wrenna. He turned to go back but Jade's firm grip on his other arm prevented him from leaving. That really disturbed him and he tried to free himself without hurting her.

"Traveller will be fine. They will bring him to our house so you'll see him then." She turned to her daughter, "Wrenna, will you go see if Dancer and Eppie can come later?"

Wrenna wanted to refuse, but after one look at her Mama's face she nodded and ran down the path that led across the valley, leaving Bish in Jade's clutches. He pulled to a stop and refused to go any further. "What the hell is going on, Jade? Where is this place? Why are all of you blue? And what's with the fangs and pointy ears? I refuse to go any further until *someone* explains *something* to me!" He stared around wildly at his surroundings. "There are things blooming! It's December. What is this place?"

Behind him, he heard Merlyn's low laughter. "Jade, I told you he was too stubborn to go, unless we explained everything first." He led his brother and wife back to the stone bench near the calm pool in the clearing. "Bish, there's no way to explain everything in a few minutes, but I'll give you the short version while Dai and the others prepare Trav so we can move him. First of all, this valley is called Mystic Valley. Our village, Lost Market is located over in that direction, past that belt of trees." He watched Bish with deep interest. "You're doing that goldfish thing again."

"But—"

"I do remember how we felt when we arrived, but trust me, you're going to have to accept some things until we have time to give you fuller explanations. Now! Where was I?" he asked Jade. "Oh, yes! There is no way out of this valley that we've been able to locate. A very few people, less than three hundred in the last thousand years, have come through that cave we found you in. Most of those have been in the last fifty years."

Bish started to say something and then thought better of it. Merlyn nodded. "Wise choice. Hmm. Dancer came through the passage about a month ago and he is bonded with our daughter, Eppie. Jade and I have fourteen children, so you're an uncle several times over… There are about fifteen hundred people in the valley, mostly in small family clans." His eyes took on an unfocused look and he stopped talking.

"What? What's going on?" Bishop demanded sharply.

Merlyn sighed. "Trouble. I had hoped to delay it for a while, but Wrenna inadvertently spilled the beans."

Jade covered her mouth with one hand and moaned. "Oh no. I didn't even think to tell her not to mention Bishop."

"Well," Merlyn said grimly, "she did, so now Dancer's enraged. You go with Bishop and Traveller back to the village.

Llyon, you take care of Traveller. Tyger, see to your Mama. Dai and I will go see Dancer and Eppie. Perhaps we can salvage the situation."

# Chapter Seventeen

ഇൗ

At Stonehollow, Dancer was repacking his bag in cold grim silence. Eppie could feel the hostility rolling off him in waves. Baffled by his anger, she tried to puzzle out exactly what had gone wrong. "Dancer, what has happened? Why are you so angry?"

"If Bishop Llewellyn is your uncle, then you have to be a Llewellyn too. I suspect that your father is the missing Baron Llewellyn?" He shot her a look so icy with contempt that she shrank back in her chair. "When were you going to tell me you're a Llewellyn?" he demanded with soft fury. "Was it something you were saving for the time I was finally so mindless with lust that I wouldn't even care?"

Shocked, she just stared at him in confusion. "I don't understand. I've always been a Llewellyn. Why does it matter?"

"Your old man knew, I told him *everything*," he flung at her bitterly. "Your grandfather killed my family. I can't prove it, but I know it. He's put a contract out on Trav and me. And now your *Uncle Bishop* has nearly succeeded in killing Trav. I knew you were too good to be true. It was all a trap, wasn't it?"

"You think we're trying to kill you? Are you insane?" she demanded heatedly.

"Who knows what you would do? God knows you bit me without asking. I should have known then! You're a Llewellyn!"

"You're so blinded by hate and grief you can't see what's in front of you!

"So tell me what I'm missing!" He tossed the challenge over his shoulder as he gathered his books from the mantel.

Angry tears trickled down her face. At the top of her lungs, she shouted, "Papa and Mama came to the valley because my grandfather tried to kill *them*. You aren't the only one he's hurt. Get in line!" Suddenly, clutching her belly, she folded up and collapsed onto the floor, whimpering in pain.

Staring at her with cold contempt, he said, "Well, that's just swell. Now you go into *schalzina* and if I don't fuck you, you'll die. Just great. I'm not sure why I even care." He went and lifted her in his arms and carried her to the bed. She slapped at his hands.

"Don't even think about touching me. I'd rather die," she snarled, not certain whether she hurt more from the *schalzina* cramps or from his angry words.

"Too bad," he said coolly, yanking off his *sharda* and blindly flinging it into the corner. "That's my child you're carrying. I won't let you die until my son or daughter's born. Until then, you'll just have to deal with it."

"If you touch me again, I'll chop that cock you're so proud of off with my knife," she threatened angrily.

"Now, we both know you won't do that," he replied contemptuously. "After all, it's the main reason you bonded with me, isn't it?" When he left her to retrieve something from his bag, she rolled off the other side of the bed. Pursing his lips together, he shook his head in disapproval and grabbed her as she ran around the bed, gently tossing her back on the soft mattress before quickly tying her hands together with the heavy sock he held in his hand. Then before she could flip over, he slipped another around the bars and secured her arms to the headboard. "Now!" he exclaimed in satisfaction as he straddled her torso. "We'll just take care of your little problem and then we'll lay down some ground rules."

She screamed in frustration and rage. "Get off me, you monster!"

"Uh-uh. Can't do that. You're all wet and swollen and ready for me. Aren't you going to give my cock a quick lick to get me harder?" he taunted.

"You stick it any nearer to me and I'll bite it off," she promised as tears dampened the hair at her temples.

"Tchk. Can't have that, can we?" He slid down between her legs so that his cock, already so hard and erect that he ached, nudged her slick, pink folds. Leaning forward, he whispered, "Ready or not, here I come," as he slid home, filling her completely in one thrust. Immediately, her *schela* clamped down, locking him into place. Abruptly, with the warm wet clasp of her pussy around his cock, horrified awareness of what his loss of control had led him to washed over him. Immediately, he tried to withdraw, but she wrapped those long, strong legs around his waist and pressed her heels into his butt preventing him from moving. They groaned in concert, though they refused to look at each other.

Without another word, in a powerful frenzy, they moved together in a bitter parody of the dance they'd performed so many times since their oath-binding. When their climaxes crashed over them, both were bitterly aware of the loss and pain both inflicted and received. Slow tears continued to wash down Eppie's face. Dancer crawled down from the bed and released her before he went into the bathing room for a warm washcloth, returning immediately to clean first Eppie's face and then between her legs. Deep in his chest, he felt the stone-cold weight of guilt mixed with shame and anger.

"Are you all right?" he demanded gruffly.

She simply shook her head, refusing to answer.

Appalled at what he had done, he gathered her in his arms, though she struggled to get away. Holding her snug against his chest, he rocked back and forth until with a final hiccupping sob, her tears stopped. "Why?" she asked in an anguished whisper.

He tucked her head beneath his chin and puzzled over his behavior. Finally, with a small shake of his head, he admitted, "I don't know. I've never done anything like that to a woman before, Eppie. Never even thought about hurting a woman."

"You didn't hurt me," she muttered. "I couldn't wait to feel your big cock stuffed in me."

"That was *schalzina*."

"I have a confession," she offered, squirming around until she could see his face.

Tilting his head back, he looked down at her. "What, another one?"

She hunched her shoulders in a little embarrassed shrug. "I want you all the time, Dancer. I wanted you desperately that very first morning at the cavern clearing. *Schalzina* was a convenient reason to tie you to me before you found someone else."

"So you weren't dying?" he asked with a frown.

"Oh, yes, that was true," she replied softly. "And it was true that we had an *attachment*. But it's also true that I don't need *schalzina* to want you. All those years waiting for you... I fell in love with you before you came."

"Did you notice how difficult it was to convince me to bond with you?" he mused with a small peculiar smile.

"What?"

"When you came through those stone sentinels, I got an instant hard-on," he said bluntly. "Yeah, yeah, I put up a little resistance, but not much. If I had truly wanted to walk away, you wouldn't have found me for years—even in a closed valley. A man just doesn't like to admit that he's been poleaxed by a six-foot blue goddess."

"Poleaxed?"

"Knocked sideways. Flattened. Stunned. You took my breath away." Very slowly, tentatively he bowed his head and kissed her, allowing her plenty of time to pull away, but she met him touch for touch in a gentle healing exploration. "I love you, Eppie," he confessed. "I think that's why I was so pissed off. When I thought you kept something like that from me, it devastated me. I'm so sorry I hurt you."

"I told you I wasn't hurt." She brushed her lips down his neck and along his shoulder, lightly nipping him with her fangs before soothing with her tongue.

"I may not have hurt you physically," he acknowledged, "but angry words hurt the heart just as much, maybe more. I made you cry."

"Well, if I had known it was Grandfather Llewellyn that killed your family, I would have told you immediately about Papa and Mama. They should have told you because they knew exactly how you would feel." Sitting up, she frowned at him. "Why didn't Papa tell you?" When she pulled away, he reluctantly released her and watched as she crawled down from the rumpled bed and located her *meerlim* and his *sharda*.

Tossing him the *sharda*, she said, "Get dressed. We're going to go to Lost Market. Wrenna said they would take Trav there. We'll go confront Papa and ask him why he didn't tell you."

Wordlessly, frowning in thought, he dressed and went to find the hairbrush while she swiftly re-braided her own hair and wound it in a small bun on top of her head. After securing it with her hair skewers, she came to him and dressed his hair in the single braid he favored.

On the path to Lost Market, they met Merlyn and Dai. Merlyn rushed toward them leaving Dai to follow more slowly. "Are you all right?" he asked Eppie. When he would have taken her into his arms, she pulled away, shifting so that Dancer was touching her back.

Dancer wrapped his arms around her and stiffly replied, "It is no thanks to you and your secrets that she's okay. I was very angry. Unfortunately, she was the only Llewellyn nearby, so she took the brunt of it. For that, I may never forgive you,

*Baron* Merlyn Llewellyn." He studied his bond father's face. "I knew you reminded me of someone. You look like Bishop. The long hair and blue skin threw me off."

"What would you have me do, Dancer? After you'd just revealed to me that my own father wiped out your entire family except for Traveller?" Merlyn paced back and forth on the narrow trail. "How was I supposed to just blurt out that 'by the way, you've ended up bonded to a Llewellyn', when clearly, you despised the very name?"

"Later? Wasn't there some time or place? Even the day you and Dai came to visit?" he demanded hotly. "What about then? Wouldn't that have been the ideal time?"

"You were hurting too bad. I couldn't add to that. Not then." He stopped in front of them. "Bishop had no part in what happened to your parents or you or Traveller. He's stunned by all that's happened to him and Trav."

"What you're asking in your convoluted way is if I'm going to kill him?" Dancer inquired in a deceptively mild tone. "No. If he agrees to a cease-fire, I'll honor it. For Eppie's sake and our child's." The hard look he sent Merlyn expressed his feelings clearly.

With a curt nod, Dai intervened. "Good. Then let us go back to Lost Market and take care of Traveller. Llyon will need assistance with healing him." He trotted away with a speed that certainly gave the lie to his seventy-plus years.

"How bad is he?" Dancer asked Merlyn, with dread.

"Very bad, but he will heal eventually. And when he wakes up, he will no doubt have even more questions that you had. Especially, when he sees those pointed ears and fangs of yours," Merlyn added straight-faced. At Dancer's appalled expression, he observed with just a touch of malice, "I guess you've been too busy to look in a mirror? You look more like a native than I do, now. All you need are the warrior braids and your own *chinkas*. You will easily pass the warrior tests." His tongue-in-cheek observation was the final straw.

As mesmerized as a snake charmer, Dancer stared at him in growing horror. Then, he glanced down at his arms wrapped around Eppie and realized the skin was indeed no longer golden, but pale blue. Almost reluctantly, he touched first one ear and then the other, tracing the gently pointed tops. Finally, he cautiously probed his teeth with one finger, tracing the elongated eyeteeth on top. "I haven't been here long enough to change," he protested in confusion.

"Perhaps, grandson, it's because you're a child of the valley." Dai paused at the next curve in the trail and cocked his head to one side, exactly like a small inquisitive bird. "Is it such a terrible thing?"

"Terrible, no," Dancer acknowledged slowly. "I knew it would happen. I suppose I just thought it would take longer to lose my identity so completely. I don't know who I am anymore. I don't look the same. I don't act the same." His bafflement was clearly written on his face.

Merlyn sighed and turned toward the village. "When Jade and I came here, it was much the same for us," he admitted. "After several years, we realized that *this* is who we were meant to be. That life back there was in reaction to the stresses my father exposed us to. *That* wasn't who we really were." He paused on the trail and earnestly regarded Dancer. "You and Traveller have been his puppets so long that you've forgotten who you were before then. Try to recall what you wanted in your life before that—what your dreams were. It might help now." With a light a shrug, he walked on with Dai, leaving Dancer and Eppie standing together in the middle of the path.

She slipped her arms around his waist and rested her head on his shoulder. "We haven't made it easy, have we?"

He pulled her tightly against his chest. "After all that I've done to you, you still try to soothe me? What have I done that I deserved you, baby?" He rubbed his chin across the top of her head, savoring the soft silky feel of her hair. "How do you suppose Traveller will feel about blue skin and pointed ears?"

"He's your brother. He will love you in all of your transformations because he loves the man at the core." She leaned back enough to look him in the eye. "Would you love me more if I looked more like an out-valley woman?"

"Hell, no!" His immediate protest shocked him as he realized that in the few short weeks he'd been in the valley, she had become the embodiment of his ideal woman. He couldn't imagine any other woman in her place. The out-valley women in his memories seemed strange and boring next to Eppie's vibrant beauty.

Reassured by his outburst, she put her head back down on his chest and sighed. "I wondered sometimes if you wished I was more like them," she admitted quietly.

He shook her gently. "Never think that, Eppie. Never, never. I'm thirty-two years old and until you, I was never even tempted to try a permanent relationship with a woman. You came into the sunlight in that clearing and my heart was plotting ways to catch you and keep you for my own. If it hadn't been *schalzina*, I would have found another way." Involuntarily, he snorted beneath his breath. "I almost had a heart attack when I realized you were naked. And then when you started yammering about a 'hard cock and full balls', you're lucky I didn't throw you down on the grass and take you right then!" He frowned at that, briefly clutched her in reaction and released her, smoothing his hands down her back.

"Much as I would like to continue this back at Stonehollow, I think we need to get to Lost Market. Something tells me that I need to be there if Traveller regains consciousness." He took her hand and trotted down the trail, urging her to hurry.

They rushed through the village to Merlyn and Jade's dome, clattering up the steps into the dark cool foyer. Dancer could hear Traveller's querulous voice demanding to "speak to their leader". Pursing his lips to suppress the grin that wanted to pop out, he tiptoed through the doorway of the treatment room, cleared his throat and asked, "Will I do?"

Traveller, obviously in pain, very slowly turned his head and studied Dancer with foggy blue eyes that moved incredulously from Dancer's face—taking in the changes in his appearance—down to his soft purple *sharda*. His eyelids fluttered closed and he moaned. "What have they done to you, Dance? You've turned into a blue Vulcan!"

Unable to contain his amusement, Dancer laughed out loud before leaning down close to Traveller's ear and murmuring, "And that's the least of it. You must get well as quickly as you can, Trav. I found my woman—and our grandfather. I have a lot to tell you once you're better."

Llyon, Dai and Merlyn worked on Trav's body with deep concentration as Mali, deep in a trance, held back the pain. Even so, he groaned when they straightened the breaks in his legs. Gritting his teeth, he cocked one eye open and took another disbelieving look at Dancer. "You're insane," he gritted out. "Certifiable."

Dancer squashed down the impulse to leap on the men working on Trav and beat them to a pulp for the pain they were causing because he *knew* they were doing their best to help him. Seeking a way to take Traveller's attention away from what was happening to him, Dance leaned back down next to his ear and said, "You're going to be an uncle. Eppie and I are going to have a baby."

"A what?" Trav just knew that his hearing must have been affected when he hit his head. He was positive Dancer couldn't be talking about babies.

"A baby. We're going to have a little blue-skinned, pointy-eared baby." Almost as an afterthought, Dancer added, "And it's half Llewellyn."

At that bit of news, it became clear to Traveller that Dancer had been thoroughly brainwashed. His eyes flew open and he stared at Dancer in consternation. Finally, he declared, "Don't worry, Dance. Just as soon as I get well, I'll save you. When we get back home, you'll feel better."

Shaking his head very slowly, Dancer inquired curiously, "Have you met your hosts, Trav? No? Allow me to introduce them, then." Gesturing at them in turn, he said, "The little guy there is our grandfather, Dai. He was Mama's papa. The fellow working on your arm is Baron Merlyn Llewellyn, Bishop's missing brother. He and his wife, Jade, have been here in this valley over twenty years." Trav twitched involuntarily as he realized that also meant that Merlyn was Free Llewellyn's son. "The young man healing your legs is Llyon Llewellyn, my bond brother and Merlyn's son. He's going to be a master healer soon," Dancer added with pride.

In spite of his pain and discomfort, Trav regarded him with growing dismay. "You've completely forgotten what they've done to our family," he panted angrily. "Well, I won't! I won't forget that they're all dead because of a Llewellyn! I won't ever forget!"

In the hallway, when Wrenna suddenly bent over and clutched her belly, Eppie and Tyger grabbed her before she could slip to the floor and eased her into a chair.

"What am I going to do now?" Wrenna whimpered.

Eppie hugged her tightly and rocked her gently. "I know. I know."

"What? What!" Tyger demanded in growing alarm as Wolfe rubbed her back and shoulders.

Worried, Eppie stared into Tyger's eyes over Wrenna's head and reminded him, "Trav is Wrenna's bond-mate. He *hates* Llewellyns. And she's begun *schalzina*."

Pursing his lips in thought, Tyger observed, "But he's not going anywhere for a while. And I have complete faith in Wrenna and her general stubbornness. In a showdown between them, my barter credits are on her."

"What will I do?" Wrenna demanded with clenched teeth.

"He's naked and can't move—the possibilities are endless. If you can't change his mind, you're not the woman I know you to be," Ty retorted with a wide grin. "I can see that

I'm going to have to build a new loom post-haste if I'm going to get your bonding blanket completed in time."

With a last pat on her shoulder, he stalked down the hall to the kitchen. "In the meantime, we're going to need more *wachaz* tea. Lots of *wachaz* tea."

*Enjoy an excerpt from:*
TRAVELLER'S REFUGE

සා

His knees cramped and he slowly straightened his long legs until they were flat on the floor. Sitting there with his back against the wall he listened intently to the storm suddenly intensify. In seconds the wailing wind was howling and shrieking around the corners of the building from the other direction. No one commented on the fact that the man who had gone to the roof had never returned. Trav hoped he had ID on him so they could identify him if they found the body.

He took a deep breath, then let it go as he pulled his legs up close to his body and wedged his size twelve Nikes flat on the floor. Damn, his ribs hurt! Tucking his bag beneath his bent knees, he leaned his head back and allowed his eyes to shut. He was so weary and a long way from home.

\* \* \* \* \*

When rescuers finally arrived, it was a damp, bedraggled group that that greeted them with dull relief. The flooding was devastating and everything in the area except the building they occupied was gone or underwater. Helicopters airlifted them from the shredded tatters of the roof—children, women and finally the remaining men. Trav was the last one hauled aboard.

When his head cleared the doorway, he found a pistol trained on him dead center. Lifting his tired eyes, he saw the face of a man he could have sworn was a friend. "Welcome aboard, nest egg," Marco said cheerfully in Cherokee.

"I'm not sure I want to," Trav replied dryly in the same language. "It doesn't sound as though the ride is going to have a happy ending for me." He noted the safety on Marco's weapon was on and flashed a glance at the others slumped in the copter. "You figure we've got ears?"

"Ears, eyes and itchy fingers." Like an Old West gunslinger, Marco twirled his pistol over his finger and settled it in the waistband of his battered jeans. "Lucky for you, I'm the one that drew this little rescue mission. Llewellyn put out a contract on you, amigo. Big bucks. Dead or alive."

Trav's gut tightened. "Dancer?"

"Did a Houdini last week. Walked right out of a concert hall in Berlin under their collective noses, carrying his violin and guitar cases. On top of that, he was dressed in his western getup complete with black cowboy hat and boots. Llewellyn is *pissed*." Marco settled back against the open doorway and pulled Trav up next to him with Trav's bag between them. "They'll be waiting for you back at the drop-off point. They have a pretty good description too. What happened to your hair?"

"I tucked it under my windbreaker."

"Fuck! I thought you cut it off! Good thing you're wearing a cap. That red hair of yours is like a beacon. You have somewhere you want us to set you down?"

"How far are you going?"

"Da Nang but they've got that sewn up good, buddy." He stared at Trav with worried eyes. "You wouldn't make it ten feet."

Trav concentrated, pitting one option against another. "Drop me at the crossroads north of Quy Nho'n," he said in sudden decision. "I'll make my own way from there."

Marco shook his head. "I'm not asking and I don't want to know. But when we get close, you better make it look good."

"No problem. I owe you a big one." Trav settled back with his eyes closed and tried to work out a plan. When they passed the outskirts of Quy Nho'n, he slipped Marco's pistol out of the man's waistband and pressed it against his ear. In careful Vietnamese, he gave him directions to set him down. Marco shouted over his shoulder to their pilot and minutes later Trav pointed to the spot where he wanted to get off. Dropping down into six inches of floodwater, he splashed to the edge of the clearing before turning to face Marco. He hurled Marco's weapon back into the chopper and

disappeared into the jungle, his mind occupied with one
burning question.

*Where was Dancer?*

# Why an electronic book?

We live in the Information Age—an exciting time in the history of human civilization, in which technology rules supreme and continues to progress in leaps and bounds every minute of every day. For a multitude of reasons, more and more avid literary fans are opting to purchase e-books instead of paper books. The question from those not yet initiated into the world of electronic reading is simply: *Why?*

1. *Price.* An electronic title at Ellora's Cave Publishing and Cerridwen Press runs anywhere from 40% to 75% less than the cover price of the exact same title in paperback format. Why? Basic mathematics and cost. It is less expensive to publish an e-book (no paper and printing, no warehousing and shipping) than it is to publish a paperback, so the savings are passed along to the consumer.

2. *Space.* Running out of room in your house for your books? That is one worry you will never have with electronic books. For a low one-time cost, you can purchase a handheld device specifically designed for e-reading. Many e-readers have large, convenient screens for viewing. Better yet, hundreds of titles can be stored within your new library—on a single microchip. There are a variety of e-readers from different manufacturers. You can also read e-books on your PC or laptop computer. (Please note that

Ellora's Cave does not endorse any specific brands. You can check our websites at www.ellorascave.com or www.cerridwenpress.com for information we make available to new consumers.)

3. *Mobility.* Because your new e-library consists of only a microchip within a small, easily transportable e-reader, your entire cache of books can be taken with you wherever you go.

4. *Personal Viewing Preferences.* Are the words you are currently reading too small? Too large? Too... ANNOYING? Paperback books cannot be modified according to personal preferences, but e-books can.

5. *Instant Gratification.* Is it the middle of the night and all the bookstores near you are closed? Are you tired of waiting days, sometimes weeks, for bookstores to ship the novels you bought? Ellora's Cave Publishing sells instantaneous downloads twenty-four hours a day, seven days a week, every day of the year. Our webstore is never closed. Our e-book delivery system is 100% automated, meaning your order is filled as soon as you pay for it.

Those are a few of the top reasons why electronic books are replacing paperbacks for many avid readers.

As always, Ellora's Cave and Cerridwen Press welcome your questions and comments. We invite you to email us at Comments@ellorascave.com or write to us directly at Ellora's Cave Publishing Inc., 1056 Home Avenue, Akron, OH 44310-3502.

# Cerridwen Press

## Monthly Newsletter

News
Author Appearances
Book Signings
New Releases
Contests
Author Profiles
Feature Articles

Available online at
www.CerridwenPress.com

# CERRIDWEN PRESS

Cerridwen, the Celtic goddess of wisdom, was the muse who brought inspiration to storytellers and those in the creative arts.

Cerridwen Press encompasses the best and most innovative stories in all genres of today's fiction.

Visit our website and discover the newest titles by talented authors who still get inspired — much like the ancient storytellers did...

once upon a time.

www.cerridwenpress.com